A HILL STATION'S VINTAGE MURDERS
AND OTHER STORIES

Ruskin Bond is known for his signature simplistic and witty writing style. He is the author of several bestselling short stories, novellas, collections, essays and children's books; and has contributed a number of poems and articles to various magazines and anthologies. At the age of 23, he won the prestigious John Llewellyn Rhys Prize for his first novel, *The Room on the Roof.* He was also the recipient of the Padma Shri in 1999, Lifetime Achievement Award by the Delhi Government in 2012 and the Padma Bhushan in 2014.

Born in 1934, Ruskin Bond grew up in Jamnagar, Shimla, New Delhi and Dehradun. Apart from three years in the UK, he has spent all his life in India and now lives in Landour, Mussoorie, with his adopted family.

RUSKIN BOND

A HILL STATION'S VINTAGE MURDERS
AND OTHER STORIES

RUPA

Published by
Rupa Publications India Pvt. Ltd 2024
7/16, Ansari Road, Daryaganj
New Delhi 110002

Sales centres:
Bengaluru Chennai
Hyderabad Jaipur Kathmandu
Kolkata Mumbai Prayagraj

P-ISBN: 978-93-6156-363-8
E-ISBN: 978-93-6156-355-3

First impression 2024

10 9 8 7 6 5 4 3 2 1

The moral right of the author has been asserted.

CONTENTS

INTRODUCTION

It is often in the most idyllic paradises that the darkest secrets lurk. It is something I have always loved about the hills—how they are both beautiful and merciless; how in their crests and troughs they hide mysteries that only add to their allure. So when these secrets are exposed to light, it is both captivating and discomfiting, like a car crash you can't look away from. After all, there is something about murder in paradise that sticks out, the way blood might on pristine snow.

A Hill Station's Vintage Murders and Other Stories is a collection of my writings that attempt to put this contrast to words, ruminating on the darker aspect of hills, and of human nature. Both 'Strychnine in the Cognac' and 'The Daryaganj Strangler' are about tourists whose darker tendencies flourish in the nooks of the mountains. 'Some Hill Station Ghosts' and 'The Bar that Time Forgot' capture the lingering, haunting spectres of people and places that hill stations are seemingly always full of. Then there are stories like 'Born Evil' and 'He Said It with Arsenic', which narrow in focus to explore the nature of the killer, and whether cruelty is not just a function of circumstance but something that runs in the blood.

I believe evil is as undeniable a part of the world as good, the way darkness is as inescapable as light. Rather than turning my eyes away from the more unsavoury aspects of life, I want to observe them just as closely as the appealing parts of it, in an attempt to understand both sides of the coin. I hope the stories herein allow you to do the same, while revelling in the inherent thrill that mysteries bring.

Ruskin Bond

STRYCHNINE IN THE COGNAC

Sick was she on Thursday,
Dead was she on Friday,
Glad was Tom on Saturday night
To bury his wife on Sunday.

Miss Bean was reclining in a cane chair in a corner of the hotel's Beer Garden, reciting old nursery rhymes to herself, when Mr Lobo, the resident pianist, walked over and placed a glass of lemon juice beside her.

'Oranges and lemons,' he said, sitting down beside her. 'Which do you prefer?'

'Both,' she said. 'Oranges for the complexion, lemons for the digestion.'

'Words of wisdom. But that nursery rhyme sounded a bit wicked. I can only remember the innocent ones like Jack and Jill.'

'Not so innocent. "Jack fell down and broke his crown"—he wouldn't have survived a broken head. Maybe Jill pushed him over a cliff—and went tumbling after!'

'Like the judge who fell into the Kempty Waterfall. Was he pushed, or did he fall?'

'We shall never know. No witnesses. But here come the Roys—what a handsome couple!'

The Roys were, indeed, a handsome couple, as you would expect them to be. Dilip Roy was in his mid-forties, but still a name to be reckoned with in Bollywood. He was greying a little at the temples, just below the edges of his wig; but he remained lean and athletic looking, and the meaty, romantic roles still came his way. His wife, Rosie Roy, was two or three years younger than him, but inclined to plumpness. When she was in her later twenties and early thirties she had starred in several very popular films—two of them opposite Dilip Roy, whom she had married while on location with him in Kashmir—but of late she had been having some difficulty in getting parts to her liking. She hadn't been feeling very well and had taken to sleeping late in the mornings. Her doctor had suspected diabetes and had advised a complete check-up, but she kept putting off the necessary tests.

'You need change,' said Dilip, always concerned about her health. 'A change from Bombay. A fortnight in the hills will do wonders for you. I'll spend a few days with you too, before I start shooting in Switzerland. Where would you like to go—Simla, Mussoorie, Darjeeling, Ooty?'

'Why not Switzerland?'

Dilip laughed uneasily. 'It wouldn't be much of a holiday. I'd be shooting all the time and you'd be pestered by hangers-on and loads of admirers.'

'Former admirers.'

'Well, better an old admirer than none at all. And I'm still jealous.'

They settled on Mussoorie—partly because Dilip Roy's father was an old friend of Nandu, the owner of the hotel, and partly because Rosie had spent an idyllic summer there as a girl, staying with an aunt in Barlowganj. When the couple arrived at the hotel, the first person they encountered was Miss Bean, watering the potted aspidistras in the porch of the hotel.

'Hello,' said Rosie, smiling curiously at Miss Bean. 'Are you the new gardener?'

'I'm the old gardener,' said Miss Bean. 'A long-time resident, actually. But the gardener never waters these aspidistras—he thinks they are hardy enough to go without. But plants are like humans—they need a little attention from time to time, otherwise they die of neglect. I've seen you somewhere, haven't I?'

'Only if you go to the movies,' said Rosie. And added: 'Old movies.'

'You're Rosie Roy,' said Miss Bean. 'I saw you in *Cobra Lady*.'

'Wasn't it terrible?'

'It was so bad that I enjoyed every moment of it. And this must be the great Dilip Roy,' observed Miss Bean as the well-known actor joined them, followed by room boys loaded with luggage. 'The hero of *Love in Kathmandu*,' said Miss Bean, but the hero ignored her.

Dilip Roy did not stop to gossip, but continued up the steps to the lobby, followed by his wife and the room boys. Miss Bean gave her attention to the aspidistras.

'Friendly heroine but not so friendly hero,' she said to the nearest potted plant. The aspidistra appeared to agree.

◆

The couple settled in, and over the next few days Miss Bean saw quite a lot of them although she took care not to intrude in any way, for it was obvious that the Roys were not looking for company.

In the evenings, Dilip Roy would plant himself on a bar stool and work his way through several whiskies, occasionally answering polite questions from the bartender or a casual customer, but always rather morosely, his mind obviously elsewhere. In the background, Mr Lobo, the hotel pianist, would play popular numbers but without receiving any encouragement or applause.

Rosie did not join her husband in the bar. But occasionally a Martini was served to her in her room—sometimes two Martinis—it was obvious that she liked a gin and vermouth cocktail now and then. Nandu presented her with a bottle of cognac, and she kept it on her dresser, intending to open it only when her husband was in the mood to drink with her.

They went out for quiet walks together, avoiding the Mall where they would quickly be recognized by both locals and visitors. Sometimes they passed Miss Bean, who was herself a great walker. As they were fellow residents of the hotel, they would stop to exchange comments on the weather, the view, the hotel, the town, sometimes even the country and the rest of the world. But from the quiet of the mountains the rest of the world can seem very far away.

Rosie Roy liked the look of Miss Bean and was always ready to stop and talk. Dilip Roy was polite but brusque. The local gossip did not interest him, and he thought Miss Bean a rather quaint and rather foolish bit of flotsam surviving from the days of the British Raj. But then (as Rosie argued) the hotel, the cottages, the winding footpaths, the hill station itself, were all survivors of the Raj, and if their old-world atmosphere did not please you, it might have been better to holiday in Goa—and soak up the Portuguese atmosphere!

India would always be haunted by its history...

◆

One day the Roys had a violent quarrel. Miss Bean was no eavesdropper but she couldn't help overhearing every word that was spoken. Her favourite place was a bench situated behind a tall hibiscus hedge. It looked out upon the snows, and Miss Bean liked to spend a half hour there with a book while Fluff, her little terrier, investigated the hillside, looking for rats' holes.

You couldn't see the bench from the Beer Garden, and it was in the Beer Garden that Rosie and Dilip Roy were confronting each other.

'You're off, because of that woman in Bandra.' Rosie's voice was quite shrill. 'A week away from her and you're beginning to look like a real Majnu—all pale and melancholy.'

'Don't make up things.' Dilip Roy sounded impatient rather than melancholy. 'You know they start shooting on the new film next week. And it's in Switzerland, not Bandra.'

'You're not the star. They can do without you. You've been getting too fat for leading roles. And you're drinking too much.'

'I'll end up an alcoholic if I stay here much longer. The doctors advised rest for you, not for me. You've given yourself ulcers and you won't get any better if you worry over trifles.'

Here the couple were interrupted by a group of youngsters seeking autographs, and Miss Bean took advantage of the diversion to slip away, taking a roundabout path to her room. Fluff enjoyed the extended walk.

That evening Dilip Roy opened the bottle of cognac. He was leaving the next morning, and he was in a mood to celebrate. But he was not particularly fond of cognac, and did most of his celebrating with his favourite Scotch. Rosie poured herself a glass of cognac, then put the bottle away on the dresser in their room. There it remained all night.

Dilip Roy breakfasted alone in the dining room, then sent for a taxi to take him down to Dehradun. Rosie did not see him off.

'She's sleeping late,' explained Dilip. 'She has a headache. Don't disturb her.'

'Enjoy yourself in Switzerland,' said Nandu, the affable proprietor.

'Look after Rosie,' said Dilip Roy. 'Let her get plenty of rest.'

And everyone did their best to make Rosie comfortable and welcome, because she was much the more gracious of the two. The manager and staff fussed over her, and Mr Lobo played her favourite tunes, especially the one she always requested:

The future is hard to see,
Whatever will be will be...

Even Miss Bean was drawn towards Rosie and joined her on an inspection of the garden, for they were both fond of flowers, and in late summer the grounds were awash with bright yellow marigolds, petunias, larkspur and climbing roses. They had coffee together and Rosie recalled her parents and happy childhood days spent in Mussoorie; she did not talk about her marriage.

As evening came on, Rosie would retire to her room and send for a Martini; it would be followed by a second. She would have a light supper in her room—usually a chicken or mushroom soup with toast—followed by a few sips of cognac as a nightcap...and then to bed.

This routine continued for three or four days, and the cognac bottle was still half full because Rosie preferred Martinis. Dilip Roy made a couple of calls from Bombay—the crew would be off to Switzerland any day, and meanwhile they were shooting some scenes in Lonavala.

He had been away for almost a week when Rosie suddenly fell ill. At about ten o'clock after her dinner she rang her bell. A room boy answered her summons, found her on her bed, still dressed, and having a fit of sorts. He ran for the manager.

The manager hurried to the room, followed by a concerned Mr Lobo. They found her still having convulsions.

'I'll go get Dr Bisht,' said Lobo, and hurried from the room. Minutes later they heard the splutter of his scooter as he took the winding driveway down to the Mall. Dr Bisht had a scooter too—it was the Age of the Scooter—and he arrived in time to give Rosie some basic first aid and arrange for her to be taken to the local hospital. He was cautious in his diagnosis. 'Looks like food poisoning,' he said, and then his eye fell on the open bottle of cognac, of which about half remained. There was still some liquor in a glass, and he sniffed at it and made a face. 'Or something else... We'd better have this bottle examined.' But that would take time.

A call was put through to Dilip Roy's studio in Bombay; but the actor was in Switzerland, and air flights were not very frequent those days. It would be two or three days before he could return.

Miss Bean visited Rosie Roy every day, and so, occasionally, did Nandu and Mr Lobo. To everyone's relief and amazement, Rosie made a good recovery. There were crystals of strychnine at the bottom of that bottle, but they had only just begun to dissolve. Another evening's drinking and Rosie would have reached the fatal dose lying in wait for her. For it was obvious that someone had placed the poison in the bottle, and that someone could only have been Dilip Roy, before he had left Mussoorie. Far away at the time of his wife's expiry, he would have the perfect alibi.

Of course, nothing could be proven—all was surmise and conjecture—but Rosie was certain in her own mind that her husband had intended to do away with her in absentia, so to speak—and had very nearly succeeded.

She and Miss Bean had become fast friends, and Rosie found herself confiding all her fears and suspicions to the older person, and turning to her for advice and guidance.

◆

They sat together on the lawns of the Savoy, Rosie reclining in an easy chair, Miss Bean quite at ease on a wooden bench. From indoors came the tinkle of a piano as Mr Lobo played 'September Song'. Miss Bean sang the words softly, almost to herself:

> *But it's a long time from May to December,*
> *And the days grown short when we reach September.*

'That's a pretty song,' said Rosie. 'A little sad, though.'

'September is a sad month,' said Miss Bean musingly. 'The end of summer, the end of all those lovely picnics. Holding hands and paddling in mountain streams. Hot sunny days. And then all that rain—weeks of endless rain and mist. September brings back the sunshine, if only for a short time, and then those icy winds will start coming down from the snows.'

'How romantic!' exclaimed Rosie. 'You are lucky to have lived here most of your life. Well, perhaps I'll come and join you when I've finished with that wretched husband of mine in Bombay.'

'What do you intend to do, my dear? Put arsenic in his vodka?'

'Arsenic is too slow. But if he eats enough of those chocolate-coated hazelnuts of which he is so fond, he could well come to a sticky end.'

'What do you mean, dear?'

'This is only for your ears, Auntie May.'

She addressed Miss Bean by her first name whenever she became trustful and confiding. 'I know you won't give me away—just in case something happens.'

'What could happen now?'

'Well, during the last two years I've been so miserable that I've always kept a little cyanide pill with me, just so that I can put an end to my life if it becomes too unbearable.'

'Oh, dear. Do throw it away. Don't even think of doing away with yourself.'

'Well, actually I did throw it away—got rid of it. I took the pill and gave it a nice coating of chocolate and then mixed it up with all the little hazelnut chocolates in the tin that Dilip always carries around.'

'Oh, but that was wicked of you. Quite diabolical! Understandable though, when you think of what he tried to do to you. But he could get to that chocolate pill any day. Pop it into his mouth, and then—'

'Pop off?' added Rosie, a glint in her hazel eyes.

'But it's been some time, hasn't it? Almost three weeks since he left. Someone else might have helped himself or herself to a chocolate—'

Just then they saw Nandu advancing across the lawn. It wasn't his usual amble, he looked very purposeful.

'Bad news,' he said, when he reached their sunny corner. 'I've just had a call from Dilip's manager. Your husband died last night. Suicide, it appears. Cyanide. He must have been feeling very guilty about what happened to you. I'm sorry for your loss, Rosie...'

♦

That evening Miss Bean dined with Rosie in the old ballroom. It was the end of the season, and only a few tables were occupied. Mr Lobo was at the piano, playing nostalgic numbers.

'What will you have, Auntie May? You're my special guest today. It's not that I want to celebrate or anything like that—'

'I quite understand, my dear.'

'So you must have a decent wine, instead of that dreadful crème-de-menthe you make in your room. Here's the wine list.'

Miss Bean ran her eye down the wine list. She was no

blackmailer, but she couldn't help feeling a little surge of power as she made her choice. And it was such a long time since she'd enjoyed a really good wine. So she plumped for the most expensive wine on the list, and sat back in anticipation.

KILLER WITH A KNIFE

Blood-red, the fallen blossoms lay on the snow, even more striking when laid bare. On the trees they blended with the foliage. On the ground, on those patches of recent snow, they seemed to be bleeding.

It had been a harsh winter in the hills, and it was still snowing at the end of March. But this was flowering time for the rhododendron trees, and they blossomed in sun, snow, or pelting rain. By mid-afternoon the hill station was shrouded in a heavy mist, and the trees stood out like ghostly sentinels.

The hill station wasn't Shimla, where I had gone to school, or Mussoorie, where I was to settle later on. It was Dalhousie, a neglected and almost forgotten hill station in the western Himalaya. But Dalhousie had the best rhododendron trees, and they grew all over the mountain, showing off before the colourless oaks and drooping pines.

But I wasn't in Dalhousie for the rhododendrons. It was 1959, and the Dalai Lama had just fled from Tibet, seeking sanctuary in India. Thousands of his followers and fellow-Tibetans had fled with him, and these refugees had to be settled somewhere. Dalhousie, with its many empty houses, was ideal for this purpose, and a carpet-weaving centre had been set up on one of the estates. The Tibetans made beautiful rugs and carpets. I know nothing about carpet-weaving, but I was working for CARE, an American relief organization, and I had been sent to Dalhousie (with the approval of the Government of India) to assess the needs of the refugees.

This is not the story of my tryst with the Tibetans, although I did suffer greatly from drinking large quantities of butter tea, which travels very slowly down the gullet and feels like lead by the time it reaches your stomach. The carpet-weaving centre became a great success, and I went on to work for CARE for several years; but that's another story. Out of one experience came another experience, as often happens during our peregrinations on planet earth, and it was during my stay in Dalhousie that I had a strange and rather unsettling experience.

I was staying at a small hotel, which was quite empty as no one visited Dalhousie in those days and certainly not at the end of March. The hill station had been convenient for visitors from Lahore, but Partition had put an end to that.

◆

The hotel had a small garden, bare at this time of the year. But on the second day of my stay, returning from the carpet-weaving centre, I noticed that there was a gardener working on the flower beds, digging around and transplanting some seedlings. He looked up as I passed, and for a moment I thought I knew him. There was something familiar about his features—the slit eyes, the broad, flattened nose, the harelip—yes, the cleft lip was very noticeable—but he wasn't anyone I knew or had known, at least I didn't think so…. He was just a likeness to someone I had seen somehow, somewhere else. It was a bit of a tease.

And it would have remained just that if he hadn't looked up and met my gaze.

A flood of recognition crossed his face. But then he looked away, almost as though he did not want to recognize me; or be recognized.

I passed him. It was curious, but it didn't bother me. We keep bumping into people who look slightly familiar. It is said that everyone has a double somewhere on this planet. I had yet to meet mine—God forbid!—but perhaps I was seeing someone else's double.

I was relaxing in the verandah later that evening, browsing through an old magazine, when the gardener passed me on his way to the garden shed to put away his tools. There was something about his walk that brought back an image from the past. He had a slight limp. And when he looked at me again, his harelip registered itself on my memory. And now I recognized him. And of course he knew me.

I was the man who'd caught him riffling through my landlady's cupboards and drawers in Dehradun, some three years previously. I had exposed him, reported him, suggested she dismiss him; but the old lady, a widow, had grown quite fond of the youth, and had kept him in her service. He was good at running about and making himself useful, and, in spite of his cleft lip, he was not unattractive.

When I left Dehradun to take up my job in Delhi, I had forgotten the matter, almost forgotten the young man and my landlady; it was another tenant who informed me that the youth—his name was Sohan—had stabbed the old lady and made off with the contents of her jewel case and other valuables. She had died in hospital a few days later.

Sohan hadn't been caught. He had obviously left the town and taken to the hills or a large city. The police had made sporadic attempts to locate him, but as time passed the case lost its urgency. The victim was not a person of importance. The criminal was a stranger, a shadowy figure of no known background.

But here he was three years later, staring me in the face. What was I to do about him? Or what was he to do about me?

◆

After Sohan had gone to his quarters, somewhere behind the hotel, I went in search of the manager. I would tell him what I knew and together we could decide on a course of action. But he had gone to a marriage and would be back late. The hotel was in charge of the cook who, a little drunk, served dinner in a hurry and retired to his quarters. 'Don't you have a night-watchman?' I asked him before he took off. 'Yes, of course,' he replied, 'Sohan, the gardener. He's the chowkidar too!'

An early retirement seemed the best thing all round, especially as I had to leave the next day. So I went to my room and made sure all the doors and windows were locked. I pushed the inside bolts all the way. I made sure the antiquated window frames were locked. As I peered out of the window, I noticed that a heavy mist had descended on the hillside. The trees stood out like ghostly apparitions, here and there a rhododendron glowing like the embers of a small fire. Then darkness enveloped the hillside. I felt cold, and wondered how much of it was fear.

I went to the bathroom and bolted the back door. Now no one could get in. Even so, I felt uneasy. Sohan was still a fugitive from the law, I had recognized him, and I was a threat to his freedom. He had killed once—perhaps more than once—and he could kill again.

I read for some time, then put out the light and tried to sleep. From a distance came the strains of music from a wedding band. Someone knocked on the door. I switched on the light and looked at my watch. It was only 10 p.m. Perhaps the manager had returned.

There was another knock, and I went to the door and was about to open it when some childhood words of warning from my grandmother came to mind: 'Never open the door unless you know who's there!'

'Who's there?' I called.

No answer. Just another knock.

'Who's there?' I called again.

There was a cough, a double-rap on the door.

'I'm sleeping,' I said. 'Come in the morning.' And I returned to my bed. The knocking continued but I ignored it, and after some time the person went away.

I slept a little. A couple of hours must have passed when I was woken by further knocking. But it did not come from the door. It was above me, high up on the wall. I'd forgotten there was a skylight.

I switched on the light and looked up. A face was outlined against the glass of the skylight. I could make out the flat rounded face and the harelip. It appeared to be grinning at me—rather like the disembodied head of the Cheshire Cat in *Alice in Wonderland*.

The skylight was very small and I knew he couldn't crawl through the opening. But he could show me a knife—and that was what he did. It was a small clasp knife and he held it between his teeth as he peered down at me. I felt very vulnerable on the bed. So I switched off the light and moved to an old sofa at the far end of the room, where I couldn't be seen. There didn't seem to be any point in shouting for help. So I just sat there, waiting.... And presumably, without a sound, he slipped away, and I remained on the sofa until the first glimmer of dawn penetrated the drawn window curtains.

◆

The manager was apologetic. 'You should have rung the bell,' he said, 'someone would have come.'

'The bell doesn't work. And someone did come...'

'I'm sorry, I'm sorry. The fellow's a villain, no doubt about it. And he's missing this morning. Your presence here must have frightened him off. So he's wanted for theft and murder. Well, we shall inform the police. Perhaps they can pick him up before he leaves the town.'

And we did inform the police. But Sohan had already taken off. The milkman had seen him boarding the early morning bus to Pathankot.

Pathankot was a busy little town on the plain below Dehradun. From there one road goes to Jammu, another to Dharamshala, a narrow-gauge railway to Kangra, and the main railway to Amritsar or Delhi. Sohan could have taken any of those routes. And no one was going to go looking for him. A police alert would be put out—a mere formality. He wasn't on their list of current criminals.

That afternoon I took a taxi to Pathankot and whiled away the evening at the railway station. My train, an overnight express to Delhi, left at 8 p.m. There was no rush at that time of the year. I had a first-class compartment to myself.

In those days our trains were somewhat different from what they are today. A first, second or third class compartment was usually a single carriage or bogey. We did not have corridor trains. Bogeys were connected by steel couplings, otherwise you were not connected in any way to the other compartments. But there was an emergency cord above the upper berths, and if you pulled it, the train might stop. There were always troublemakers on the trains, just as there are today, and sometimes the chain was pulled out of mischief. As a result it was often ignored.

As the train began moving out of the station I went to all the windows and made sure that they were fastened. Then I bolted the carriage door. I was becoming adept at bolting doors and windows. Sohan was probably hiding out in some distant town or village, but I wasn't taking any chances.

The train gathered speed. The lights of Pathankot receded as we plunged into a dark and moonless night. I had a pillow and a blanket with me, and I stretched out on one of the bunks and tried to think about pleasant things such as scarlet geraniums, fragrant sweet peas, and the beautiful Nimmi, star of the silver screen; but instead I kept seeing the grinning face of a young man with a harelip. All the same, I drifted into sleep. The rocking movement of the carriage, the rhythm of the wheels on the rails, have always had a soothing effect on my nerves. I sleep well in trains and rocking chairs.

But not that night.

I woke to the sound of that familiar tapping; not at the door, but on the window glass not far from my head. The insistent tapping of someone who wanted to get in.

It was common enough for ticketless travellers to hang on to the carriage of a moving train, in the hope that someone would let them in. But they usually chose the crowded second or third-class compartments; a first-class traveller, often alone, was unlikely to let in a stranger who might well turn out to be a train robber.

I raised my head from my pillow, and there he was, clinging to the fast-moving train, his face pressed to the glass, his harelip revealing part of a broken tooth.... I pulled down the shutters, blotting out his face. But, agile as a cat, he moved to the next window, the sneer still on his face. I pulled down that shutter too.

I pulled down all the shutters on his side of the carriage. He couldn't get in, bodily. But mentally, he was all over me.

Mind over matter. Well, I could apply my mind too. I shut my eyes and willed my tormentor to fall off the train!

No one fell off the train (at least no one was reported to have done so), but presently we slowed to a gradual stop and, when I pulled up the shutters of the window, I saw that we were at a station. Jalandhar, I think. The platform was brightly lit and there was no sign of Sohan. He must have jumped off the train as it slowed down. It was about one in the morning. A vendor brought me a welcome glass of hot tea, and life returned to normal.

◆

I did not see Sohan in the years that followed. Or rather, I saw many Sohans. For two or three years I was pursued by my 'familiar'. Wherever I went—and my work took me to different parts of the country—I found myself encountering young men with harelips and a menacing look. Pure imagination, of course. He had every reason to stay as far from me as possible.

Gradually, the 'sightings' died down. Young men with harelips became extremely rare. Perhaps they were all going in for corrective surgery.

The years passed, and I had forgotten my familiar. I had given up my job in Delhi and moved to the hills. I was a moderately successful writer, and a familiar figure on Mussoorie's Mall Road. Sometimes other writers came to see me in my cottage under the deodars. One of them invited me to have dinner with him at the old Regal hotel, where he was staying. Before dinner, he took me to the bar for a drink.

'What will you have, whisky or vodka?'

No one seemed to drink anything else. I asked for some dark rum, and the barman went off in search of a bottle. When he returned and began pouring my drink, I noticed something slightly familiar about his features, his stance. He was almost bald, and he had a grey, drooping moustache which concealed most of his upper lip. He glanced at me and our eyes met. There was no sign of recognition. He smiled politely as he poured my drink. No, it definitely wasn't Sohan. He was too refined, for one thing. And he went about his duties without another glance in my direction.

Dinner over, I thanked my writer friend for his hospitality, and took the long walk home to my cottage. It was a dark, moonless night. No one followed me, no one came tapping on my bedroom window.

◆

Mussoorie had its charms. In my mind, every hill station is symbolized by a particular tree, even if it's not the dominant one. Dalhousie has its rhododendrons, Shimla its deodars, Kasauli its pines and Mussoorie its horse chestnuts. The monkeys would do their best to destroy the chestnuts, but I would collect those that were whole and plant them in people's gardens, whether they wanted them or not. The horse chestnut is a lovely tree to look at, even if you can't do anything with it!

My walks took me to the Regal from time to time, and occasionally I would relax in the bar, chatting to an old resident or a casual visitor, while the barman poured me a rum and soda. He never looked twice at me. And I never saw him outside that bar room. He appeared to be as much of a fixture as the moth-eaten antler-head on the wall, only he wasn't quite as moth-eaten.

'Efficient chap,' said Colonel Bhushan indicating the barman. 'And a great favourite with his mistress.'

'You mean the owner of this place?' I had only a vague idea of who owned what in the town. And in some cases the ownership was rather vague. But in the case of the Regal—Mrs Kapoor, a wealthy widow in her fifties, was very much in charge, all too visible an owner; well fleshed-out, ample-bosomed, with arms like rolling pins. Her staff trembled at her approach; but not, it seemed, the bartender, who led a charmed life, incapable of doing any wrong.

The lights went out, as they frequently do in this technological age, and the barman brought over our next round of drinks by candlelight.

By the light of a candle I caught a glimpse of the barman's features as he hovered over me. There was only the hint of a harelip, and the candle lit up his slanting eyes and prominent cheekbones. This was the only time I had a really close look at him.

◆

A week later I met Colonel Bhushan on the Mall. This was where all the gossip took place.

'Have you heard what happened last night at the Regal?' He wasted no time in getting to the news of the day.

A twinge of fear, of anticipation, ran through me. 'Nothing too terrible, I hope?'

'That barman chap—always thought he was a bit too smooth—stabbed the old lady, stabbed her two or three times, then plundered her room and made off with jewellery worth lakhs—as well as all the cash he could find!'

'How's the lady?'

'She'll survive. Tough old buffalo. But the rascal got away. By now he must be in Sirmur, or even across the Nepal border. Probably belongs to some criminal tribe.'

Yes, I thought, possibly a descendant of one of those robber gangs who harassed pilgrims on their way to the sacred shrines, or plundered traders from Tibet, or caravans to Samarkand.... To rob and plunder still runs in the blood of the most harmless looking people.

So the barman at the Regal was the same man I'd known in Dehradun and then encountered in Dalhousie. The passing of time had altered his features but not his way of life. By now he would probably be far from Mussoorie. But I had a feeling I'd see him again—if not here, then somewhere else. Each one of us had a 'familiar'—a presence we would rather do without—an unwelcome and menacing guest—and for me it is Sohan.

Where does he come from, where does he go? I doubt if I shall ever know.

But I have a feeling he'll turn up again one of these days. And then?

A CASE FOR INSPECTOR LAL

I met Inspector Keemat Lal about two years ago, while I was living in the hot, dusty town of Shahpur in the plains of northern India.

Keemat Lal had charge of the local police station. He was a heavily built man, slow and rather ponderous, and inclined to be lazy; but, like most lazy people, he was intelligent. He was also a failure. He had remained an Inspector for a number of years, and had given up all hopes of a further promotion. His luck was against him, he said. He should never have been a policeman. He had been born under the sign of Capricorn and should really have gone into the restaurant business; but now it was too late to do anything about it.

The Inspector and I had little in common. He was nearing forty, and I was twenty-five. But both of us spoke English, and in Shahpur there were very few people who did. In addition, we were both fond of beer. There were no places of entertainment in Shahpur. The searing heat, the dust that came whirling up from the east, the mosquitoes (almost as numerous as the flies), and the general monotony gave one a thirst for something more substantial than stale lemonade.

My house was on the outskirts of the town, where we were often not disturbed. On two or three evenings in the week, just as the sun was going down and making it possible for one to emerge from the khas-cooled confines of a dark, high-ceilinged bedroom, Inspector Keemat Lal would appear on the verandah steps, mopping the sweat from his face with a small towel, which he used instead of a handkerchief. My only servant, excited at the prospect of serving an inspector of police, would hurry out with glasses, a bucket of ice and several bottles of the best Indian beer.

One evening, after we had overtaken our fourth bottle, I said, 'You must have had some interesting cases in your career, Inspector.'

'Most of them were rather dull,' he said. 'At least the successful ones were. The sensational cases usually went unsolved—otherwise I might have been a superintendent by now. I suppose you are talking of murder cases. Do you remember the shooting of the Minister of the Interior? I was on that one, but it was a political murder and we never solved it.'

'Tell me about a case you solved,' I said. 'An interesting one.' When I saw him looking uncomfortable, I added, 'You don't have to worry, Inspector. I'm a very discreet person, in spite of all the beer I consume.'

'But how can you be discreet? You are a writer.'

I protested: 'Writers are usually very discreet. They always change the names of people and places.'

He gave me one of his rare smiles. 'And how would you describe me, if you were to put me into a story?'

'Oh, I'd leave you as you are. No one would believe in you, anyway.'

He laughed indulgently and poured out more beer. 'I suppose I can change names, too... I will tell you a very interesting case. The victim was an unusual person, and so was the killer. But you must promise not to write this story.'

'I promise,' I lied.

'Do you know Panauli?'

'In the hills? Yes, I have been there once or twice.'

'Good, then you will follow me without my having to be too descriptive. This happened about three years ago, shortly after I had been stationed at Panauli. Nothing much ever happened there. There were a few cases of theft and cheating, and an occasional fight during the summer. A murder took place about once every ten years. It was, therefore, quite an event when the Rani of — was found dead in her sitting-room, her head split open by an axe. I knew that I would have to solve the case if I wanted to stay in Panauli.

'The trouble was, anyone could have killed the Rani, and there were some who made no secret of their satisfaction that she was dead. She had been an unpopular woman. Her husband was dead, her children were scattered, and her money—for she had never been a very wealthy Rani—had been dwindling away. She lived alone in an old house on the outskirts of the town, ruling the locality with the stern authority of a matriarch. She had a servant, and he was the man who found the body and came to the police, dithering and tongue-tied. I arrested him at once, of course. I knew he was probably innocent, but a basic rule is to grab the first man on the scene of the crime, especially if he happens to be a servant. But we let him go after a beating. There was nothing much he could tell us, and he had a sound alibi.

'The axe with which the Rani had been killed must have been a small woodcutter's axe—so we deduced from the wound. We couldn't find the weapon. It might have been used by a man or a woman, and there were several of both sexes who had a grudge against the Rani. There were bazaar rumours that she had been supplementing her income by trafficking in young women: she had the necessary connections. There were also rumours that she possessed vast wealth, and that it was stored away in her godowns. We did not find any treasure. There were so many rumours darting about like battered shuttlecocks that I decided to stop wasting my time in trying to follow them up. Instead I restricted my enquiries to those people who had been close to the Rani—either in their personal relationships or in actual physical proximity.

'To begin with, there was Mr Kapur, a wealthy businessman from Bombay who had a house in Panauli. He was supposed to be an old admirer of the Rani's. I discovered that he had occasionally lent her money, and that, in spite of his professed friendship for her, he had charged a high rate of interest.

'Then there were her immediate neighbours—an American missionary and his wife, who had been trying to convert the Rani to Christianity; an English spinster of seventy who made no secret of the fact that she and the Rani had hated each other with great enthusiasm; a local councillor and his family, who did not get on well with their aristocratic neighbour; and a tailor, who kept his shop close by. None of these people had any powerful motive for killing the Rani—or none that I could discover. But the tailor's daughter interested me.

'Her name was Kusum. She was twelve or thirteen years old—a thin dark girl, with lovely black eyes and a swift, disarming smile. While I was making my routine enquiries in the vicinity of the Rani's house, I noticed that the girl always tried to avoid me. When I questioned her about the Rani, and about her own movements on the day of the crime, she pretended to be very vague and stupid.

'But I could see she was not stupid, and I became convinced that she knew something unusual about the Rani. She might even know something about the murder. She could have been protecting someone, and was afraid to tell me what she knew. Often, when I spoke to her of the violence of the Rani's death, I saw fear in her eyes. I began to think the girl's life might be in danger, and I had a close watch kept on her. I liked her. I liked her youth and freshness and the innocence and wonder in her eyes. I spoke to her whenever I could, kindly and paternally, and though I knew she rather liked me and found me amusing—the ups and downs of Panauli always left me panting for breath—and though I could see that she *wanted* to tell me something, she always held back at the last moment.

'Then, one afternoon while I was in the Rani's house going through her effects, I saw something glistening in a narrow crack near the doorstep. I would not have noticed it if the sun had not been pouring through the window, glinting off the little object. I stooped and picked up a piece of glass. It was part of a broken bangle.

'I turned the fragment over in my hand. There was something familiar about its colour and design. Didn't Kusum wear similar glass bangles? I went to look for the girl but she was not at her father's shop. I was told that she had gone down the hill, to gather firewood.

'I decided to take the narrow path down the hill. It went round some rocks and cactus, and then disappeared into a forest of oak trees. I found Kusum sitting at the edge of the forest, a bundle of twigs beside her.

'"You are always wandering about alone," I said. "Don't you feel afraid?"

'"It is safer when I am alone," she replied. "Nobody comes here."

'I glanced quickly at the bangles on her wrist, and noticed that their colour matched that of the broken piece. I held out the bit of broken glass and said, "I found it in the Rani's house. It must have fallen…"

'She did not wait for me to finish what I was saying. With a look of terror, she sprang up from the grass and fled into the forest.

'I was completely taken aback. I had not expected such a reaction. Of what significance was the broken bangle? I hurried after the girl, slipping on the smooth pine needles that covered the slopes. I was searching amongst the trees when I heard someone sobbing behind me. When I turned round, I saw the girl standing on a boulder, facing me with an axe in her hands.

'When Kusum saw me staring at her, she raised the axe and rushed down the slope towards me.

'I was too bewildered to be able to do anything but stare with open mouth as she rushed at me with the axe. The impetus of her run would have brought her right up against me, and the axe, coming down, would probably have crushed my skull, thick though it is. But while she was still six feet from me, the axe flew out of her hands. It sprang into the air as though it had a life of its own and came curving towards me.

'In spite of my weight, I moved swiftly aside. The axe grazed my shoulder and sank into the soft bark of the tree behind me. And Kusum dropped at my feet, weeping hysterically.'

Inspector Keemat Lal paused in order to replenish his glass. He took a long pull at the beer, and the froth glistened on his moustache.

'And then what happened?' I prompted him.

'Perhaps it could only have happened in India—and to a person like me,' he said. 'This sudden compassion for the person you are supposed to destroy. Instead of being furious and outraged, instead of seizing the girl and marching her off to the police station, I stroked her head and said silly comforting things.'

'And she told you that she had killed the Rani?'

'She told me how the Rani had called her to her house and given her tea and sweets. Mr Kapur had been there. After some time he began stroking Kusum's arms and squeezing her knees. She had drawn away, but Kapur kept pawing her. The Rani was telling Kusum not to be afraid, that no harm would come to her. Kusum slipped away from the man and made a rush for the door. The Rani caught her by the shoulders and pushed her back into the room. The Rani was getting angry. Kusum saw the axe lying in a corner of the room. She seized it, raised it above her head and threatened Kapur. The man realized that he had gone too far, and, valuing his neck, backed away. But the Rani, in a great rage, sprang at the girl. And Kusum, in desperation and panic, brought the axe down across the Rani's head.'

'The Rani fell to the ground. Without waiting to see what Kapur might do, Kusum fled from the house. Her bangle must have broken when she stumbled against the door. She ran into the forest and, after concealing the axe amongst some tall ferns, lay weeping on the grass until it grew dark. But such was her nature, and such the resilience of youth, that she recovered sufficiently to be able to return home looking her normal self. And during the following days she managed to remain silent about the whole business.'

'What did you do about it?' I asked.

Keemat Lal looked me straight in my beery eye.

'Nothing,' he said. 'I did absolutely nothing. I couldn't have the girl put away in a remand home. It would have crushed her spirit.'

'And what about Kapur?'

'Oh, he had his own reasons for remaining quiet, as you may guess. No, the case was closed—or perhaps I should say the file was put in my pending tray. My promotion, too, went into the pending tray.'

'It didn't turn out very well for you,' I said.

'No. Here I am in Shahpur, and still an Inspector. But, tell me, what would you have done if you had been in my place?'

I considered his question carefully for a moment or two, then said, 'I suppose it would have depended on how much sympathy the girl evoked in me. She had killed in innocence...'

'Then you would have put your personal feelings above your duty to uphold the law?'

'Yes. But I would not have made a very good policeman.'

'Exactly.'

'Still, it's a pity that Kapur got off so easily.'

'There was no alternative if I was to let the girl go. But he didn't get off altogether. He found himself in trouble later for swindling some manufacturing concern, and went to jail for a couple of years.'

'And the girl—did you see her again?'

'Well, before I was transferred from Panauli, I saw her occasionally on the road. She was usually on her way to school. She would greet me with joined palms, and call me Uncle.'

The beer bottles were all empty, and Inspector Keemat Lal got up to leave. His final words to me were, 'I should never have been a policeman.'

HE SAID IT WITH ARSENIC

Is there such a person as a born murderer—in the sense that there are born writers and musicians, born winners and losers? One can't be sure. The urge to do away with troublesome people is common to most of us but only a few succumb to it.

If ever there was a born murderer, he must surely have been William Jones. The thing came so naturally to him. No extreme violence, no messy shootings or hacking or throttling. Just the right amount of poison, administered with skill and discretion.

A gentle, civilized sort of person was Mr Jones. He collected butterflies and arranged them systematically in glass cases. His ether bottle was quick and painless. He never stuck pins into the beautiful creatures.

Have you ever heard of the Agra Double Murder? It happened, of course, a great many years ago, when Agra was a far-flung outpost of the British Empire. In those days, William Jones was a male nurse in one of the city's hospitals. The patients—especially terminal cases—spoke highly of the care and consideration he showed them. While most nurses, both male and female, preferred to attend to the more hopeful cases, Nurse William was always prepared to stand duty over a dying patient.

He felt a certain empathy for the dying. He liked to see them on their way. It was just his good nature, of course.

On a visit to nearby Meerut, he met and fell in love with

Mrs Browning, the wife of the local stationmaster. Impassioned love letters were soon putting a strain on the Agra–Meerut postal service. The envelopes grew heavier—not so much because the letters were growing longer but because they contained little packets of a powdery white substance, accompanied by detailed instructions as to its correct administration.

Mr Browning, an unassuming and trustful man—one of the world's born losers, in fact—was not the sort to read his wife's correspondence. Even when he was seized by frequent attacks of colic, he put them down to an impure water supply. He recovered from one bout of vomitting and diarrhoea only to be racked by another.

He was hospitalized on a diagnosis of gastroenteritis. And, thus freed from his wife's ministrations, soon got better. But on returning home and drinking a glass of nimbu paani brought to him by the solicitous Mrs Browning, he had a relapse from which he did not recover.

Those were the days when deaths from cholera and related diseases were only too common in India and death certificates were easier to obtain than dog licences.

After a short interval of mourning (it was the hot weather and you couldn't wear black for long) Mrs Browning moved to Agra where she rented a house next door to William Jones.

I forgot to mention that Mr Jones was also married. His wife was an insignificant creature, no match for a genius like William. Before the hot weather was over, the dreaded cholera had taken her too. The way was clear for the lovers to unite in holy matrimony.

But Dame Gossip lived in Agra, too, and it was not long before tongues were wagging and anonymous letters were being received by the superintendent of police. Inquiries were instituted. Like most infatuated lovers, Mrs Browning had hung on to her beloved's letters and *billet doux*, and these soon came to light. The silly woman had kept them in a box beneath her bed.

Exhumations were ordered in both Agra and Meerut. Arsenic keeps well, even in the hottest of weather, and there was no dearth of it in the remains of both victims.

Mr Jones and Mrs Browning were arrested and charged with murder.

'Is Uncle Bill really a murderer?' I asked from the drawing-room sofa in my grandmother's house in Dehra. (It's time I told you that William Jones was my uncle, my mother's half-brother.)

I was eight or nine at the time. Uncle Bill had spent the previous summer with us in Dehra and had stuffed me with bazaar sweets and pastries, all of which I had consumed without suffering any ill effects.

'Who told you that about Uncle Bill?' asked Grandmother.

'I heard it in school. All the boys are asking me the same question—"Is your uncle a murderer?" They say he poisoned both his wives.'

'He had only one wife,' snapped Aunt Mabel.

'Did he poison her?'

'No, of course not. How can you say such a thing!'

'Then why is Uncle Bill in gaol?'

'Who says he's in gaol?'

'The boys at school. They heard it from their parents. Uncle Bill is to go on trial in the Agra fort.'

There was a pregnant silence in the drawing room, then Aunt Mabel burst out: 'It was all that awful woman's fault.'

'Do you mean Mrs Browning?' asked Grandmother.

'Yes, of course. She must have put him up to it. Bill couldn't have thought of anything so—so diabolical!'

'But he sent her the powders, dear. And don't forget—

Mrs Browning has since…'

Grandmother stopped in mid-sentence and both she and Aunt Mabel glanced surreptitiously at me.

'Committed suicide,' I filled in. 'There were still some powders with her.'

Aunt Mabel's eyes rolled heavenwards. 'This boy is impossible. I don't know what he will be like when he grows up.'

'At least I won't be like Uncle Bill,' I said. 'Fancy poisoning people! If I kill anyone, it will be in a fair fight. I suppose they'll hang uncle?'

'Oh, I hope not!'

Grandmother was silent. Uncle Bill was her stepson but she did have a soft spot for him. Aunt Mabel, his sister, thought he was wonderful. I had always considered him to be a bit soft but had to admit that he was generous. I tried to imagine him dangling at the end of a hangman's rope but somehow he didn't fit the picture.

As things turned out, he didn't hang. White people in India seldom got the death sentence, although the hangman was pretty busy disposing of dacoits and political terrorists. Uncle Bill was given a life sentence and settled down to a sedentary job in the prison library at Naini, near Allahabad. His gifts as a male nurse went unappreciated. They did not trust him in the hospital.

He was released after seven or eight years, shortly after the country became an independent republic. He came out of jail to find that the British were leaving, either for England or the remaining colonies. Grandmother was dead. Aunt Mabel and her husband had settled in South Africa. Uncle Bill realized that there was little future for him in India and followed his sister out to Johannesburg. I was in my last year at boarding school. After my father's death, my mother had married an Indian and now my future lay in India.

I did not see Uncle Bill after his release from prison and no one dreamt that he would ever turn up again in India.

In fact, fifteen years were to pass before he came back, and by then I was in my early thirties, the author of a book that had become something of a bestseller. The previous fifteen years had been a struggle—the sort of struggle that every young freelance writer experiences—but at last the hard work was paying off and the royalties were beginning to come in.

I was living in a small cottage on the outskirts of the hill station of Fosterganj, working on another book, when I received an unexpected visitor.

He was a thin, stooped, grey-haired man in his late fifties with a straggling moustache and discoloured teeth. He looked feeble and harmless but for his eyes, which were a pale cold blue. There was something slightly familiar about him.

'Don't you remember me?' he asked. 'Not that I really expect you to, after all these years...'

'Wait a minute. Did you teach me at school?'

'No—but you're getting warm.' He put his suitcase down and I glimpsed his name on the airlines label. I looked up in astonishment. 'You're not—you couldn't be...'

'Your Uncle Bill,' he said with a grin and extended his hand. 'None other!' And he sauntered into the house.

I must admit that I had mixed feelings about his arrival. While I had never felt any dislike for him, I hadn't exactly approved of what he had done. Poisoning, I felt, was a particularly reprehensible way of getting rid of inconvenient people. Not that I could think of any commendable ways of getting rid of them! Still, it had happened a long time ago, he'd been punished, and presumably he was a reformed character.

'And what have you been doing all these years?' he asked me, easing himself into the only comfortable chair in the room.

'Oh, just writing,' I said.

'Yes, I heard about your last book. It's quite a success, isn't it?'

'It's doing quite well. Have you read it?'

'I don't do much reading.'

'And what have you been doing all these years, Uncle Bill?'

'Oh, knocking about here and there. Worked for a soft drink company for some time. And then with a drug firm. My knowledge of chemicals was useful.'

'Weren't you with Aunt Mabel in South Africa?'

'I saw quite a lot of her until she died a couple of years ago. Didn't you know?'

'No. I've been out of touch with relatives.' I hoped he'd take that as a hint. 'And what about her husband?'

'Died too, not long after. Not many of us left, my boy. That's why, when I saw something about you in the papers, I thought—why not go and see my only nephew again?'

'You're welcome to stay a few days,' I said quickly. 'Then I have to go to Bombay.' (This was a lie but I did not relish the prospect of looking after Uncle Bill for the rest of his days.)

'Oh, I won't be staying long,' he said. 'I've got a bit of money put by in Johannesburg. It's just that—so far as I know—you're my only living relative and I thought it would be nice to see you again.'

Feeling relieved, I set about trying to make Uncle Bill as comfortable as possible. I gave him my bedroom and turned the window seat into a bed for myself. I was a hopeless cook but, using all my ingenuity, I scrambled some eggs for supper. He waved aside my apologies. He'd always been a frugal eater, he said. Eight years in jail had given him a cast-iron stomach.

He did not get in my way but left me to my writing and my lonely walks. He seemed content to sit in the spring sunshine and smoke his pipe.

It was during our third evening together that he said, 'Oh, I almost forgot. There's a bottle of sherry in my suitcase. I brought it especially for you.'

'That was very thoughtful of you, Uncle Bill. How did you know I was fond of sherry?'

'Just my intuition. You do like it, don't you?'

'There's nothing like a good sherry.'

He went to his bedroom and came back with an unopened bottle of South African sherry.

'Now you just relax near the fire,' he said agreeably. 'I'll open the bottle and fetch glasses.'

He went to the kitchen while I remained near the electric fire, flipping through some journals. It seemed to me that Uncle Bill was taking rather a long time. Intuition must be a family trait because it came to me quite suddenly—the thought that Uncle Bill might be intending to poison me.

After all, I thought, here he is after nearly fifteen years, apparently for purely sentimental reasons. But I had just published a bestseller. And I was his nearest relative. If I was to die Uncle Bill could lay claim to my estate and probably live comfortably on my royalties for the next five or six years!

What had really happened to Aunt Mabel and her husband, I wondered. And where did Uncle Bill get the money for an air ticket to India?

Before I could ask myself any more questions, he reappeared with the glasses on a tray. He set the tray on a small table that stood between us. The glasses had been filled. The sherry sparkled.

I stared at the glass nearest me, trying to make out if the liquid in it was cloudier than that in the other glass. But there appeared to be no difference.

I decided I would not take any chances. It was a round

tray, made of smooth Kashmiri walnut wood. I turned it round with my index finger, so that the glasses changed places.

'Why did you do that?' asked Uncle Bill.

'It's a custom in these parts. You turn the tray with the sun, a complete revolution. It brings good luck.'

Uncle Bill looked thoughtful for a few moments, then said, 'Well, let's have some more luck,' and turned the tray around again.

'Now you've spoilt it,' I said. 'You're not supposed to keep revolving it! That's bad luck. I'll have to turn it about again to cancel out the bad luck.'

The tray swung round once more and Uncle Bill had the glass that was meant for me.

'Cheers!' I said and drank from my glass.

It was good sherry.

Uncle Bill hesitated. Then he shrugged, said 'Cheers' and drained his glass quickly.

But he did not offer to fill the glasses again.

Early next morning he was taken violently ill. I heard him retching in his room and I got up and went to see if there was anything I could do. He was groaning, his head hanging over the side of the bed. I brought him a basin and a jug of water.

'Would you like me to fetch a doctor?' I asked.

He shook his head. 'No, I'll be all right. It must be something I ate.'

'It's probably the water. It's not too good at this time of the year. Many people come down with gastric trouble during their first few days in Fosterganj.'

'Ah, that must be it,' he said and doubled up as a fresh spasm of pain and nausea swept over him.

He was better by evening—whatever had gone into the glass must have been by way of the preliminary dose and a day later he was well enough to pack his suitcase and announce his departure.

The climate of Fosterganj did not agree with him, he told me.

Just before he left, I said: 'Tell me, Uncle, why did you drink it?'

'Drink what? The water?'

'No, the glass of sherry into which you'd slipped one of your famous powders.'

He gaped at me, then gave a nervous whinnying laugh. 'You will have your little joke, won't you?'

'No, I mean it,' I said. 'Why did you drink the stuff? It was meant for me, of course.'

He looked down at his shoes, then gave a little shrug and turned away.

'In the circumstances,' he said, 'it seemed the only decent thing to do.'

I'll say this for Uncle Bill: he was always the perfect gentleman.

A JOB WELL DONE

Dhuki, the gardener, was clearing up the weeds that grew in profusion around the old disused well. He was an old man, skinny and bent and spindly-legged; but he had always been like that; his strength lay in his wrists and in his long, tendril-like fingers. He looked as frail as a petunia, but he had the tenacity of a vine.

'Are you going to cover the well?' I asked. I was eight, a great favourite of Dhuki. He had been the gardener long before my birth; had worked for my father, until my father died, and now worked for my mother and stepfather.

'I must cover it, I suppose,' said Dhuki. 'That's what the "Major sahib" wants. He'll be back any day, and if he finds the well still uncovered, he'll get into one of his raging fits and I'll be looking for another job!'

The 'Major sahib' was my stepfather, Major Summerskill. A tall, hearty, back-slapping man, who liked polo and pig-sticking. He was quite unlike my father. My father had always given me books to read. The Major said I would become a dreamer if I read too much, and took the books away. I hated him and did not think much of my mother for marrying him.

'The boy's too soft,' I heard him tell my mother. 'I must see that he gets riding lessons.'

But before the riding lessons could be arranged, the Major's regiment was ordered to Peshawar. Trouble was expected from some of the frontier tribes. He was away for about two months. Before leaving, he had left strict instructions for Dhuki to cover up the old well.

'Too damned dangerous having an open well in the middle of the garden,' my stepfather had said. 'Make sure that it's completely covered by the time I get back.'

Dhuki was loath to cover up the old well. It had been there for over fifty years, long before the house had been built. In its walls lived a colony of pigeons. Their soft cooing filled the garden with a lovely sound. And during the hot, dry summer months, when taps ran dry, the well was always a dependable source of water. The *bhisti* still used it, filling his goatskin bag with the cool clear water and sprinkling the paths around the house to keep the dust down.

Dhuki pleaded with my mother to let him leave the well uncovered.

'What will happen to the pigeons?' he asked.

'Oh, surely they can find another well,' said my mother. 'Do close it up soon, Dhuki. I don't want the Sahib to come back and find that you haven't done anything about it.'

My mother seemed just a little bit afraid of the Major. How can we be afraid of those we love? It was a question that puzzled me then, and puzzles me still.

The Major's absence made life pleasant again. I returned to my books, spent long hours in my favourite banyan tree, ate buckets of mangoes, and dawdled in the garden talking to Dhuki.

Neither he nor I were looking forward to the Major's return. Dhuki had stayed on after my mother's second marriage only out of loyalty to her and affection for me; he had really been my father's man. But my mother had always appeared deceptively frail and helpless, and most men, Major Summerskill included, felt protective towards her. She liked people who did things for her.

'Your father liked this well,' said Dhuki. 'He would often sit here in the evenings, with a book in which he made drawings of birds and flowers and insects.'

I remembered those drawings, and I remembered how they had all been thrown away by the Major when he had moved into the house. Dhuki knew about it, too. I didn't keep much from him.

'It's a sad business closing this well,' said Dhuki again. 'Only a fool or a drunkard is likely to fall into it.'

But he had made his preparations. Planks of sal wood, bricks and cement were neatly piled up around the well.

'Tomorrow,' said Dhuki. 'Tomorrow I will do it. Not today. Let the birds remain for one more day. In the morning, Baba, you can help me drive the birds from the well.'

On the day my stepfather was expected back, my mother hired a tonga and went to the bazaar to do some shopping. Only a few people had cars in those days. Even colonels went about in tongas. Now, a clerk finds it beneath his dignity to sit in one.

As the Major was not expected before evening, I decided I would make full use of my last free morning. I took all my favourite books and stored them away in an outhouse where I could come for them from time to time. Then, my pockets bursting with mangoes, I climbed into the banyan tree. It was the darkest and coolest place on a hot day in June.

From behind the screen of leaves that concealed me, I could see Dhuki moving about near the well. He appeared to be most unwilling to get on with the job of covering it up.

'Baba!' he called, several times; but I did not feel like stirring from the banyan tree. Dhuki grasped a long plank of wood and placed it across one end of the well. He started hammering. From my vantage point in the banyan tree, he looked very bent and old.

A jingle of tonga bells and the squeak of unoiled wheels told me that a tonga was coming in at the gate. It was too early for my mother to be back. I peered through the thick, waxy leaves of the tree, and nearly fell off my branch in surprise. It was my stepfather, the Major! He had arrived earlier than expected.

I did not come down from the tree. I had no intention of confronting my stepfather until my mother returned.

The Major had climbed down from the tonga and was watching his luggage being carried onto the verandah. He was red in the face and the ends of his handlebar moustache were stiff with brilliantine. Dhuki approached with a half-hearted salaam.

'Ah, so there you are, you old scoundrel!' exclaimed the Major, trying to sound friendly and jocular. 'More jungle than garden, from what I can see. You're getting too old for this sort of work, Dhuki. Time to retire! And where's the Memsahib?'

'Gone to the bazaar,' said Dhuki.

'And the boy?'

Dhuki shrugged. 'I have not seen the boy today, Sahib.'

'Damn!' said the Major. 'A fine homecoming, this is. Well, wake up the cook-boy and tell him to get some sodas.'

'Cook-boy's gone away,' said Dhuki.

'Well, I'll be double-damned,' said the Major.

The tonga went away, and the Major started pacing up and down the garden path. Then he saw Dhuki's unfinished work at the well. He grew purple in the face, strode across to the well, and started ranting at the old gardener.

Dhuki began making excuses. He said something about a shortage of bricks; the sickness of a niece; unsatisfactory cement; unfavourable weather; unfavourable gods. When none of this seemed to satisfy the Major, Dhuki began mumbling about something bubbling up from the bottom of the well, and pointed down into its depths. The Major stepped on to the low parapet and looked down. Dhuki kept pointing. The Major leant over a little.

Dhuki's hands moved swiftly, like a conjurer's making a pass. He did not actually push the Major. He appeared merely to tap him once on the bottom. I caught a glimpse of my stepfather's boots as he disappeared into the well. I couldn't help thinking of Alice in Wonderland, of Alice disappearing down the rabbit hole.

There was a tremendous splash, and the pigeons flew up, circling the well thrice before settling on the roof of the bungalow.

By lunch time—or tiffin, as we called it then—Dhuki had the well covered over with the wooden planks.

'The Major will be pleased,' said my mother, when she came home. 'It will be quite ready by evening, won't it, Dhuki?'

By evening, the well had been completely bricked over. It was the fastest bit of work Dhuki had ever done.

Over the next few weeks, my mother's concern changed to anxiety, her anxiety to melancholy, and her melancholy to resignation. By being gay and high-spirited myself, I hope I did something to cheer her up. She had written to the Colonel of the Regiment, and had been informed that the Major had gone home on leave a fortnight previously. Somewhere, in the vastness of India, the Major had disappeared.

It was easy enough to disappear and never be found. After several months had passed without the Major turning up, it was presumed that one of two things must have happened. Either he had been murdered on the train, and his corpse flung into a river; or, he had run away with a tribal girl and was living in some remote corner of the country.

Life had to carry on for the rest of us. The rains were over, and the guava season was approaching.

My mother was receiving visits from a colonel of His

Majesty's 32nd Foot. He was an elderly, easy-going, seemingly absent-minded man, who didn't get in the way at all, but left slabs of chocolate lying around the house.

'A *good* Sahib,' observed Dhuki, as I stood beside him behind the bougainvillea, watching the colonel saunter up the verandah steps. 'See how well he wears his sola topi! It covers his head completely.'

'He's bald underneath,' I said.

'No matter. I think he will be all right.'

'And if he isn't,' I said, 'we can always open up the well again.'

Dhuki dropped the nozzle of the hosepipe, and water gushed out over our feet. But he recovered quickly and, taking me by the hand, led me across to the old well, now surmounted by a three-tiered cement platform which looked rather like a wedding cake.

'We must not forget our old well,' he said. 'Let us make it beautiful, Baba. Some flower pots, perhaps.'

And together we fetched pots, and decorated the covered well with ferns and geraniums. Everyone congratulated Dhuki on the fine job he'd done. My only regret was that the pigeons had gone away.

A HILL STATION'S VINTAGE MURDERS

There is less crime in the hills than in the plains, and so the few murders that do take place from time to time stand out as landmarks in the annals of a hill station.

Among the gravestones in the Mussoorie cemetery there is one that bears the inscription: 'Murdered by the hand he befriended.' This is the grave of Mr James Reginald Clapp, a chemist's assistant, who was brutally done to death on the night of 31 August 1909.

Miss Ripley-Bean, who has spent most of her eighty-seven years in this hill station, remembers the case clearly, though she was only a girl at the time. From the details she has given me, and from a brief account in *A Mussoorie Miscellany*, now out of print, I am able to reconstruct this interesting case and a couple of others that were the sensations of their respective 'seasons'.

Mr Clapp was an assistant in the chemist's shop of Messrs. J.B. & E. Samuel (no longer in existence), situated in one of the busiest sections of the Mall. At that time the adjoining cantonment of Landour was an important convalescent centre for British soldiers. Mr Clapp was popular with the soldiers, and he had befriended some of them when they had run short of money. He was a steady worker and sent most of his savings home, to his mother in Birmingham; she was planning to use the money to buy the house in which she lived.

At the time of the murder, Clapp was particularly friendly with a Corporal Allen, who was eventually to be hanged at the Naini Jail. The murder was brutal, the initial attack being launched with a soda-water bottle on the victim's head. Clapp's throat was then cut from ear to ear with his own razor, which was left behind in the room. The body was discovered on the floor of the shop the next morning by the proprietor, Mr Samuel, who did not live on the premises.

Suspicion immediately fell on Corporal Allen because he had left Mussoorie that same night, arriving at Rajpur, in the foothills (a seven-mile walk by the bridle path) many hours later than he was expected at a Rajpur boarding-house. According to some, Clapp had last been seen in the corporal's company.

There was other circumstantial evidence pointing to Allen's guilt. On the day of the murder, Mr Clapp had received his salary, and this sum, in sovereigns and notes, was never traced. Allen was alleged to have made a payment in sovereigns at Rajpur. Someone had given Allen a biscuit tin packed with sandwiches for his journey down, and it was thought that perhaps the tin had been used by the murderer as a safe for the money. But no tin was found, and Allen denied having had one with him.

Allen was arrested at Rajpur and brought back to Mussoorie under escort. He was taken immediately to the victim's bedside, where the body still lay, the police hoping that he might confess his guilt when confronted with the body of the victim; but Allen was unmoved, and protested his innocence.

Meanwhile, other soldiers from among Mr Clapp's friends had collected on the Mall. They had removed their belts and were ready to lynch Allen as soon as he was brought out of the shop. The situation was tense, but further mishap was averted by the resourcefulness of Mr Rust, a photographer, who, being of the same build as the corporal, put on an army coat with a turned-up collar, and arranged to be handcuffed between two policemen. He remained with them inside the shop, in partial view of the mob, while the rest of the police party escorted the corporal out by a back entrance. Mr Rust did not abandon his disguise or leave the shop until word arrived that Allen was secure in the police station.

Corporal Allen was eventually found guilty, and was hanged. But there were many who felt that he had never really been proved guilty, and that he had been convicted on purely circumstantial evidence; and looking back on the case from this distance in time one cannot help feeling that the soldier may have been a victim of circumstances, and perhaps of local prejudice, for he was not liked by his fellows. Allen himself hinted that he was not in the vicinity of the crime that night but in the company of a lady whose integrity he was determined to shield. If this was true, it was a pity that the lady prized her virtue more than her friend's life, for she did not come forward to save him. The chaplain who administered to Allen during his last days in the 'condemned cell' was prepared to absolve the corporal and could not accept that he was a murderer.

One of the hill station's most sensational crimes was committed on 25 July 1927, at the height of the 'season' and in the heart of the town, in Zephyr Hall, then a boarding-house. It provided a good deal of excitement for the residents of the boarding-house.

Soon after midday, Zephyr Hall residents were startled into brisk activity when a woman screamed and a shot rang out from one of the rooms. Other shots followed in rapid succession.

Those boarders who happened to be in the public lounge or verandah dived for the safety of their rooms; but one unhappy resident, taking the precaution of coming around a corner with his hands held well above his head, ran straight into a levelled pistol. And the man with the gun, who had just killed his wife and wounded his daughter, was still able to see some humour in the situation, for he burst into laughter! The boarder escaped unhurt. But the murderer, Mr Owen, did not savour the situation for long. He shot himself long before the police arrived.

Ten years earlier, on 24 November 1917, another husband had shot his wife.

Mrs Fennimore, the wife of a schoolmaster, had got herself inextricably enmeshed in a defamation law suit, each hearing of which was more distasteful to Mr Fennimore than the previous one. Finally he determined on his own solution. Late at night he armed himself with a loaded revolver, moved to his wife's bedside, and, finding her lying asleep on her side, shot her through the back of the head. For no accountable reason he put the weapon under her pillow, and then completed his plan. Going to the lavatory, three rooms beyond his wife's bedroom, he leaned over his loaded rifle and shot himself.

THE SKELETON IN THE CUPBOARD

Yes, there was a skeleton in the cupboard, and although I never saw it, I played a small part in the events that followed its discovery.

I was fifteen that year, and back in my boarding school in Shimla after spending the long winter holidays in Dehradun. My mother was still managing the old Green's Hotel in Dehra—a hotel that was soon to disappear and become part of Dehra's unrecorded history. It was called Green's not because it purported to spread any greenery (its neglected garden was choked with lantana), but because it had been started by an Englishman, Mr Green, back in 1920, just after the Great War had ended in Europe. Mr Green had died at the outset of World War II. He had just sold the hotel and was on his way back to England when the ship on which he was travelling was torpedoed by a German submarine. Mr Green went down with the ship.

The hotel had already been in decline and the new owner, a Sikh businessman from Ludhiana, had done his best to keep it going. But in the wake of the War and India's newly won independence, Dehra was going through a lean period. My stepfather's motor workshop was also going through a lean period—a crisis, in fact—and my mother was glad to take the job of running the small hotel, while he took a job in Delhi.

She wrote to me about once a month, giving me news of the hotel, some of its more interesting guests and the pictures that were showing in town.

'I know you're interested in detective stories,' she wrote during the summer term,

> and that you fancy yourself a Sherlock Holmes or Ellery Queen. So what do you make of this strange happening? Last week we decided to clear out an old storeroom that hadn't been opened for years. The keys were missing, so we had to break open the lock. Inside there was a lot of old furniture, rotting carpets, dusty files, broken flowerpots, even a mounted tiger's head. There were two or three locked cupboards which had to be forced open. Nothing much in the first two, but the third cupboard gave everyone a fright. As Tirloki, our billiard marker, pulled open the door, a skeleton tumbled out! I mean a complete human skeleton! It must have been there for twenty years or more. How did it get there, and why? If you were here, you could do some detective work, but you'll have to wait for the winter holidays. Of course, we had to inform the police, and they took the skeleton away, saying they'd have it examined. But I doubt if they'll do much about it. It's obviously someone who died long ago—perhaps a hotel guest!—and someone here decided to hush it up. Suicide? Murder? Accident? Probably we'll never know…

Well, boy-detective that I fancied myself, I wrote back to my mother and said, 'I'll solve the case when I come home. But was it a man's skeleton, or a woman's? And did you find anything else in the cupboard?'

A week later my mother wrote back:

> I didn't look too closely at the skeleton—I like bones to be fully-fleshed if possible—but the police did say it was

a woman. Not an old woman, and not too young either.
There was nothing else in the cupboard except for some
chipped or cracked plates and dishes, which have now
been thrown away. The shelves were covered with sheets
of old newspapers. I've kept those for you.

The newspapers excited me, and I wrote and asked my mother
for some details.

She wrote back:

I hope you're preparing for your exams. After all, there's
not much we can do about a skeleton that's been hidden
away for fifteen or twenty years. Anyway, there were
two newspapers in the cupboard. The *Daily Chronicle*,
published from Delhi on 18 January 1930, is complete.
That was four years before you were born. The main
headline refers to the 'Bareilly Train Disaster' in which
thirteen passengers were killed and nineteen seriously
injured. There are also two pages of book reviews,
including a review of *The Glenlitten Murder* by E. Phillips
Oppenheim. I think you may have read some of his
books. He wrote that story 'Crooks in the Sunshine', if
you remember.

The other book is about the spirit world, and the
possibility of communicating with those who have passed
from this material world. Perhaps we can summon up
the spirit of the person who inhabited the skeleton? She
could tell us how she met her end. Old Miss Kellner
holds séances and table-rappings. But how would she
summon up a spirit if she doesn't know who it was in
the first place?

The second newspaper—incomplete—is *The Civil and
Military Gazette* of 2 March 1930. This was published from

Lahore, and as you know, Mr Kipling worked on it a few years earlier. The front page is missing, but page 5 carries an ad for a film called *The Awakening of Love* starring Vilma Bank. Vilma was a popular heroine when I was a girl. Nothing much else of interest except for a small item under the headline, 'Elder Murder Sequel':

Patna, Feb. 28: The Chief Justice and Mr Justice Scroope have dismissed the appeal of O.W. Harrison, who was charged with the murder of Mr W.P. Elder in July and confirmed the sentence of death passed on him by the Sessions Judge of Manbhum.

Nothing to do with our skeleton, of course, because Mr Elder was buried at Jamshedpur, while Harrison occupies an unknown grave. And in any case our skeleton is a woman's. But I remember the case. Harrison was having an affair with Mr Elder's wife. When confronted by the outraged husband, Harrison took out his revolver and shot the poor man. All very sordid. No mystery there for you. Concentrate on your studies. Second-term exams must be near. I am sending you a parcel of socks. I know they don't last very long on you.

Two weeks later I wrote:

Dear Mum,

Thanks for the socks. But I wish you had sent me a food parcel instead. How about some guava cheese? And some mango pickle. They don't give us pickle in school. Headmaster's wife says it heats the blood.

About that skeleton. If a dead body was hidden in that cupboard after 1930—must have been, if the newspapers of that year were under the skeleton—it must have been someone who disappeared around that time or a little later. Must have been before Tirloki joined the hotel or he'd remember. What about the hotel registers—would they give us a clue?

I soon received a parcel containing guava cheese, strawberry jam and mango pickle. Headmaster confiscated the pickle. Maybe he needed it to heat his blood.

A note enclosed with the parcel read:

Old hotel registers missing. Must have been thrown out. Or perhaps Mr Green took them away when he left. Tirloki says a German spy stayed in the hotel just before the War broke out. The spy used to visit the Gurkha lines and the armaments factory. He was passing information on to a dentist who visited Germany every year. When the War broke out, the dentist was kept in a prisoner-of-war camp. The spy disappeared—some say to Tibet. Could the spy have been silenced and put away in the cupboard? But I keep forgetting it was a woman's skeleton. Tirloki says the spy was a man. But a clever spy may have been a woman dressed as a man. What do you think?

It was the football season, and I wasn't doing much thinking. Chasing a football in the monsoon mist and slush called for single-minded endurance, especially when we were being beaten 5–0 by the Shimla Youngs, a team of junior clerks from the government offices. Not the ideal training for a boy-detective. The winter holidays were still four months distant, and the case of the unidentified skeleton appeared to be resolving itself with a little help from my mother and her friends.

'Well, I went to see Miss Kellner,' wrote my mother a few weeks later,

You know, the crippled old lady who used to be your Granny's tenant. She had me over for tea, and we talked about the old days, and what a good place Green's Hotel used to be—famous for its food and service and flower garden. Mr Green was a great one for the ladies. Very dapper and handsome. Women couldn't resist his charm, his polished manner, and he could dance! A great dancer, like Fred Astaire. Ballroom dancing, of course. None of your rumbas or sambas or jitterbugging.

'And what of Mrs Green?' I asked. 'He was married, wasn't he?'

'Poor Mrs Green,' said Miss Kellner, 'she had to put up with his amours and affairs. A quiet person, she came from a good English family. He'd married her for her money, of course. Her father owned hotels in Brighton. Green talked him into financing a couple of hotels in India. One in Poona, one in Dehra. This was a promising place then. Europeans wanted to settle here. But once married, Green neglected his wife. He fancied himself a Don Juan, and carried on with several women.'

'So did she leave him?' I asked.

'No one really knew what happened,' said Miss Kellner. 'Mrs Green just disappeared. It was all a great mystery, and of course there were all sorts of rumours. You see, if she'd just walked out on him she'd have told someone, confided in a friend. She did have a few friends. I like to think I was one of them. We were all expecting her to leave Green, but no one knew where she went or when. There were no letters, no postcards. Green gave out that she'd gone to stay with friends in Bombay, but after a six-month absence, speculation was rife. And no one believed she'd taken off with another man—she wasn't the sort.'

'And what about her father,' I asked Miss Kellner. 'Didn't he come looking for her?'

'Indeed, he did,' said Miss Kellner. 'She hadn't been in touch with him, and she hadn't returned to England as far as he knew.'

Apparently, he made enquiries all over India—no one had seen her or heard from her. So he spoke to the few friends she had in Dehra, including Miss Kellner. They only confirmed his suspicions, that she had been done away with—but how and where? He reported her disappearance to the police, but there was little they could do except question Mr Green, who maintained that he was just as mystified as anyone else and offered a large reward to anyone who could locate her! By then, of course, everyone was convinced that she was dead, and that Green had done away with her, or paid someone to do the dirty work.

Several years passed, and then Green sold up and went away. 'And deserved to go down with the ship,' added Miss Kellner. 'That was the general opinion.'

When I told Miss Kellner about the skeleton in the cupboard, she was certain that it was Mrs Green's.

He must have strangled her or poisoned her, and then locked the body in that cupboard in the storeroom. Only he had the key to the stores.

I've spoken to Padre Dutt and one or two others who were here at the time, and they are all convinced that the skeleton is Mrs Green's. What can we do about it now? So many years have passed, and her old father is long dead. She did not have any children. If there were distant relatives it would be almost impossible to trace them after all this time. Padre Dutt thinks we should give

the skeleton a Christian burial, on the strong assumption
that it's Mrs Green.

The mystery of the skeleton in the cupboard appeared to have
been solved without the assistance of boy-detective Ruskin. I
tried to forget it and concentrate on chemistry and mathematics,
but I'm afraid I was spending more and more time perusing the
works of Agatha Christie, Rex Stout and Raymond Chandler—
and trying to write a detective story in which our Headmaster
was found bludgeoned to death in the science lab.

My mother brought me up to date on events in Dehra.

Padre Dutt managed to retrieve the skeleton from police
custody, and it was interred in a corner of the cemetery,
not far from your grandfather's grave. I attended the
funeral with two or three other old-timers who had known
the Greens. Miss Kellner is bedridden now and could
not come. Padre Dutt is getting on too, and is a little
absent-minded.

It was raining heavily during the funeral service and
by mistake he read out the 'Burial at Sea'. Not that anyone
seemed to notice. Anyway, he had arranged for a decent
coffin, and there's to be a tombstone too, paid for out of
church funds and with a contribution from our Sardar-ji,
the present owner of the hotel. So poor Mrs Green has
found a final resting place. May she rest in peace!

And there the matter rested until the school term ended and I
came home for my holidays.

◆

My mother was still managing Green's, even though its days
were numbered. The day after my return, I joined her in the

small office, where she sat behind her overlarge desk, telephone on her right, a tin of Gold Flake (her favourite cigarette) on her left, and the latest paperback western before her, ready to be taken up when nothing much was happening—which was fairly often. My mother enjoyed reading westerns—particularly Luke Short, Max Brand and Clarence E. Mulford—much in the same way that I enjoyed detective fiction. Both genres were freely available in cheap Collins White Circle editions published during and just after the War.

We discussed the affair of the skeleton in the cupboard, but as there was no longer any mystery about it, there was nothing for me to investigate. However, armed with the keys to the storeroom, I went down to the basement on my own and made a thorough search of all the old furniture, on the off-chance that another skeleton might tumble out of a cupboard or be found jammed into a drawer or trunk. I did find some old tennis racquets, back numbers of *Punch*, a cracked china chamberpot, some old postcards of Darjeeling and Shimla, and a framed photograph of King Edward VII. I took the copies of *Punch* to my room, and read the reviews of all the plays that had been running in London between 1926 and 1930, thus becoming an authority on the theatre in England of that period.

'No more skeletons,' I remarked to my mother in the office, two or three days later.

'How disappointing,' she said. 'And the one we did find is not only dead, it's buried. Why don't you join a cricket team?'

'Snooker is more exciting. Tirloki is teaching me.'

'I hope he isn't teaching you to smoke and drink.'

'When did you start smoking, Mum?'

'None of your business.'

Someone was standing in the doorway. An elderly woman, very fluffy, very pink. Her cheeks were pink, her dress was pink, her hair was bunched up and white. She was straight out of Agatha Christie.

'Miss Marple!' I exclaimed.

'May I come in?' asked the pink lady.

'Please come in,' said my mother. 'Do sit down. Do you require a room?'

'Not today, thank you. I'm staying with Padre Dutt. He insisted on putting me up. But I may want a room for a day or two—just for old times' sake.'

'You've stayed here before?'

'A long time ago. I'm Mrs Green, you know. The missing Mrs Green. The one for whom you put up that handsome tombstone in the cemetery. I was very touched by it. And I'm glad you didn't add "Beloved Wife of Henry Green", because I didn't love him any more than he loved me.'

'Then—then—you aren't the skeleton?' stammered my mother.

'Do I look like a skeleton?'

'No!' we said together.

'But we heard you disappeared,' I said, 'and when we found that skeleton—'

'You put two and two together.'

'Well, it was Miss Kellner who convinced us,' said my mother. 'And you did disappear mysteriously. You were missing for years. And everyone knew Mr Green was a philanderer.'

'Couldn't wait to get away from him,' said the pink lady. 'Couldn't stand him any more. He was a ladykiller, but not a *real* killer.'

'But your father came looking for you. Didn't you get in touch with him?'

'My father and I were never very close. Mother died when I was very young, and the only relative I had was a cousin in

West Africa. So that's where I went—Sierra Leone!'

'How romantic!' said my mother.

'It's hot and steamy in Sierra Leone,' said Mrs Green. 'But the climate does wonders for your libido. I lived in sin with a wonderful black man for several years.'

'What happened to him?' I asked, conjuring up a picture of a small pink woman and a large black man having sex together. At fifteen, the imagination is swamped by erotic images.

'He was killed in a tribal war,' said Mrs Green without any show of emotion. 'It was a long time ago.'

'And that skeleton,' I asked. 'What about the skeleton in the cupboard? Did you know about it?'

'Yes, I knew about it. But I have no idea whose skeleton it was. You see, back in the 1920s, when Green took over this hotel, he had one of his sudden enthusiasms and was convinced this town needed a medical school or college, and he set about preparing the ground for one. He was ready to finance the project or part of it. And of course medical students need a skeleton. So he acquired one from the Lady Hardinge Medical College in New Delhi. It was a medical-school skeleton you found. And if you'd looked closely, you'd have noticed that it was varnished.'

'Why was it varnished?' I asked.

'To help preserve it, of course. It was also articulated.'

'Articulated?'

'That means the joints were connected up, so that the whole thing wouldn't fall apart. Want to be a doctor, young man?'

'No,' I said. 'A detective.'

'Well, you didn't solve this case.'

'I wasn't here. And now we'll never be able to identify the skeleton.'

'Some poor woman of the streets, no doubt. Unclaimed, unwanted. But in the end you gave her a decent burial—even if she wasn't a Christian. Padre Dutt is a bit embarrassed, but I've told him I don't mind my name on the tombstone. I'll be returning to Africa shortly, and when I die I shall have another tombstone there. Not everyone is lucky enough to have two tombstones!'

And with that she made a graceful exit from our lives.

IN A CRYSTAL BALL:
A MUSSOORIE MYSTERY

Conan Doyle, the creator of Sherlock Holmes, had a lifelong interest in unusual criminal cases, and his friends often passed on to him interesting accounts of crime and detection from around the world. It was in this way that he learnt of the strange death of Miss Frances Garnett-Orme in the Indian hill station of Mussoorie. Here was a murder combining the weird borders of the occult with a crime mystery as inexplicable as any devised by Doyle himself.

In April 1912 (shortly before the *Titanic* went down), Conan Doyle received a letter from his Sussex neighbour Rudyard Kipling:

Dear Doyle,

There has been a murder in India. A murder by suggestion at Mussoorie, which is one of the most curious things in its line on record.

Everything that is improbable and on the face of it impossible is in this case.

Kipling had received details of the case from a friend working in the Allahabad *Pioneer*, a paper for which, as a young man, he had worked in the 1880s. Urging Doyle to pursue the story, Kipling concluded: 'The psychology alone is beyond description.'

Doyle was indeed interested to hear more, for India had furnished him with material in the past, as in *The Sign of Four* and several short stories. Kipling, too, had turned to crime and detection in his early stories of Strickland of the Indian Police. The two writers got together and discussed the case, which was indeed a fascinating affair.

The scene was set in Mussoorie, a popular hill station in the foothills of the Himalayas. It wasn't as grand as Simla (where the Viceroy and his entourage went) but it was a charming and convivial place, with a number of hotels and boarding houses, a small military cantonment, and several private schools for European children.

It was during the summer 'season' of 1911 that Miss Frances Garnett-Orme came to stay in Mussoorie, taking a suite at the Savoy, a popular resort hotel. On 28 July she celebrated her 49th birthday. She was the daughter of George Garnett-Orme, of Skipton-in-Craven in Yorkshire, a district registrar of the Country Court. It was a family important enough to be counted among the landed gentry. Her father had died in 1892.

She came out to India in 1893 with the intention of marrying Jack Grant of the United Provinces Police. But he died in 1894 and she went back to England. Upset by his death following so soon after her father's, she turned to spiritualism in the hope of communicating with him. We must remember that spiritualism was all the rage in the early years of the century, seances and table-rappings being part of the social scene both in England and India. Madam Blavatsky, the chief exponent of spiritualism, was probably at the height of her popularity around this time; she spent her 'seasons' in neighbouring Simla, where she had many followers.

Miss Garnett-Orme's life was unsettled. She was drawn back to India, returning in 1901 to live in Lucknow, the regional capital of the United Provinces. She was still in contact with Jack Grant's family and saw his brother occasionally. The summer of 1907 was spent at Nainital, a hill station popular with Lucknow residents. It was here that she met Miss Eva Mountstephen, who was working as a governess.

Eva Mountstephen, too, had an interest in spiritualism. It appears that she had actually told several of her friends about this time that she had learnt (in the course of a seance) that in 1911 she would come into a great deal of money.

We are told that there was something sinister about Miss Mountstephen. She specialized in crystal-gazing, and what she saw in the glass often took a violent form. Her 'control', that is her connection in the spirit world, was a dead friend named Mrs Winter.

As a result of their common interest in the occult, Miss Garnett-Orme took on the younger woman as a companion when she returned to Lucknow in the winter. There they settled down together. But the summers were spent at one of the various hill stations. Was there a latent lesbianism in their relationship? It was a restless, rootless life, but they were held together by the strong and heady influence of the seance table and the crystal ball. Miss Garnett-Orme's indifferent health also made her dependent on the younger woman.

In the summer of 1911, the couple went up to Mussoorie, probably the most frivolous of hill stations, where 'seasonal' love affairs were almost the order of the day. They took rooms in the Savoy. Electricity had yet to reach Mussoorie, and it was still the age of candelabras and gas-lit streets. Every house had a grand piano. If you didn't go out to a ball, you sang or danced at home. But Miss Garnett-Orme's spiritual pursuits took precedence over these more mundane entertainments. Towards the end of the 'season', on 12 September, Miss Mountstephen returned to Lucknow to pack up their household for a move to Jhansi, where they planned to spend the winter.

On the morning of 19 September, while Miss Mountstephen was still away, Miss Garnett-Orme was found dead in her bed. The door was locked from the inside. On her bedside table was a glass. She was positioned on the bed as though laid out by a nurse or undertaker.

Because of these puzzling circumstances, Major Birdwood of the Indian Medical Service (who was the Civil Surgeon in Mussoorie) was called in. He decided to hold an autopsy. It was discovered that Miss Garnett-Orme had been poisoned with prussic acid.

Prussic acid is a quick-acting poison, and would have killed too quickly for the victim to have composed herself in the way she was found. An ayah told the police that she had seen someone (she could not tell whether it was a man or a woman) slipping away through a large skylight and escaping over the roof.

Hill stations are hotbeds of rumour and intrigue, and of course the gossips had a field day. Miss Garnett-Orme suffered from dyspepsia and was always dosing herself from a large bottle of Sodium Bicarbonate, which was regularly refilled. It was alleged that the bottle had been tampered with, that an unknown white powder had been added. Her doctor was questioned thoroughly. They even questioned a touring mind-reader, Mr Alfred Capper, who claimed that Miss Mountstephen had hurried from a room rather than have her mind read!

After several weeks the police arrested Miss Mountstephen. Although she had a convincing alibi (due to her absence in Jhansi) the police sought to prove that some kind of sinister influence had been exerted on Miss Garnett-Orme to take her medicine at a particular time. Thus, through suggestion, the murderer could kill and yet be away at the time of death. In her first novel, *The Mysterious Affair at Styles* (1920), the poisoner was in a distant place by the time her victim reached the fatal dose, the poison having precipitated to the bottom of the mixture. Perhaps Miss Christie read accounts of the Garnett-Orme case in the British press. Even the motive was similar.

But there was no Hercule Poirot in Mussoorie, and in court this theory could never be made convincing. The police case was never strong (they would have done better to have followed the ayah's lead), and it appears that they only acted because there was considerable ill-feeling in Mussoorie against Miss Mountstephen.

When the trial came up at Allahabad in March 1912, it caused a sensation. Murder by remote control was something new in the annals of crime. But after hearing many days of evidence about the ladies' way of life, about crystal-gazing and premonitions of death, the court found Miss Mountstephen innocent. The Chief Justice, in delivering his verdict, remarked that the true circumstances of Miss Garnett-Orme's death would probably never be known. And he was right.

Miss Mountstephen applied for probate of her friend's will. But the Garnett-Orme family in England sent out her brother, Mr Hunter Garnett-Orme, to contest it. The case went in favour of Mr Garnett-Orme. The District Judge (W.D. Burkitt) turned down Miss Mountstephen's application on grounds of 'fraud and undue influence in connection with spiritualism and crystal-gazing'. She went in appeal to the Allahabad High Court, but the Lower Court's decision was upheld.

Miss Mountstephen returned to England. We do not know her state of mind, but if she was innocent, she must have been a deeply embittered woman. Miss Garnett-Orme's doctor lost his flourishing practice in Mussoorie and left the country too. There were rumours that he and Miss Mountstephen had conspired to get hold of Miss Garnett-Orme's considerable fortune.

There was one more puzzling feature of the case. Mr Charles Jackson, a painter friend of many of those involved, had died suddenly, apparently of cholera, two months after Miss Garnett-Orme's mysterious death. The police took an interest in his sudden demise. When he was exhumed on 23 December, the body was found to be in a perfect state of preservation. He had died of arsenic poisoning.

Murder or suicide? This puzzle, too, was never resolved. Was there a connection with Miss Garnett-Orme's death? That too we shall never know. Had Conan Doyle taken up Kipling's suggestion and involved himself in the case (as he had done in so many others in England), perhaps the outcome would have been different.

As it is, we can only make our own conjectures.

THE BAR THAT TIME FORGOT

'Cockroaches!' exclaimed Her Highness the Maharani. 'Cockroaches everywhere! Can't put down my glass without finding a cockroach beneath it!'

'Cockroaches have a special liking for this room,' observed Colonel Wilkie, from his corner by the disused fireplace. 'For one thing, our Melaram there'—and he indicated the bartender with a tilt of his double chin—'never washes the glasses properly. And there are sandwich remains all over the place. Last week's sandwiches, I might add. From that party of yours, Krishan.'

Krishan, former Test cricketer, now forty and with a forty-three-inch waist, turned to the colonel. 'You should see the kitchen. A pigsty. The cook is seldom sober.'

'*We* are seldom sober,' said Suresh Mathur, income-tax lawyer, from his favourite bar stool.

'Speak for yourself,' snapped H.H. 'Simon, fetch me another whisky.'

Simon Lee, secretary-companion to Her Highness, rose dutifully from his chair and took her glass over to the bar counter.

'Indian whisky or Scotch, sir?' asked the bartender in a loud voice, knowing the Maharani was too mean to buy Scotch.

'Whisky will do,' said Simon. 'And a beer for me.' Just then he felt like spiking the Maharani's whisky with something really lethal, and be free of her for the rest of his days. Years of loyalty and companionship had given way to abject slavery, and there was nothing he could do about it. Nearing seventy, unqualified and unworldly, he could hardly set about creating any sort of career for himself.

'And what are *you* having?' he asked Suresh Mathur, who had just put away his first drink.

'I am never vague, I ask for Haig!' Suresh replied, chuckling at his clever rhyme. None of the others thought it amusing, but this was usual. 'When they stop giving me credit, I'll try the local stuff.'

'Good on you!' called Colonel Wilkie from his corner. 'But there's nothing to beat Solan No. 1. Don't trust these single malts—they always give one gout!'

'I've never seen you move from that chair,' said Krishan. 'No wonder you suffer from gout.'

'Played cricket once, like you,' said the Colonel. 'Made a few runs. But they always made me twelfth man. Got fed up of carrying out the drinks, or fielding when the star batsman felt indisposed. Gave up cricket. Indoor games are better. Why don't we have a dartboard in here? In England, every respectable pub has a dartboard.'

I'd been listening to the conversation from a small table behind a potted palm. I was sixteen, just out of school, and I wasn't supposed to be in the bar, even if I wasn't drinking. The large potted palm separated the bar-room from the outer lounge; it was neutral territory.

'I have a dartboard!' I piped up, and every head turned towards me. Most of them had been unaware of my presence. They knew, of course, that I was the son of the lady who managed the hotel.

Suresh Mathur, the most literary-inclined of the lot, said: 'Young Copperfield has a dartboard!'

'I'll go and fetch it,' I said, only too ready to justify my presence in the bar.

I dashed down the corridor to my room and collided with my mother who was doing her nightly round of the hotel.

'What are you doing here? You mustn't hang around the bar,' she said sharply. 'You have a radio in your room, apart from all your books.'

The radio had been given to me the previous year by a guest who was now wanted by the police (on suspicion of being a serial killer), but I did not feel in any way guilty about possessing it; the guest had been very friendly and generous.

'Darts,' I told my mother. 'They want to play darts. That's what a pub is for, isn't it?' And I charged into my room, picked up my old dartboard and set of darts, and returned breathless to the bar-room.

My arrival was greeted by cheers, and Krishan helped me find a place for the dartboard, just below a framed picture of winged cherubs sporting about on some unlikely clouds.

'Whoever gets the highest score gets a free drink,' announced Krishan.

'Who pays for it?' asked Suresh Mathur.

'We all do—income-tax lawyers included.'

'He never saved anyone a rupee of tax,' declared the Maharani. 'But come on, let's have a game.'

'Would you like to start the proceedings, H.H.?'

'No, I'll wait till everyone's finished. You can start with Colonel Wilkie.'

'Age before beauty,' said Krishan. 'Come on, Colonel, we know you have a steady hand.'

Colonel Wilkie's hand was far from steady. His hands were always trembling. But he struggled out of his chair and took up his position at a point indicated by Krishan. Only one of his darts struck the board, earning him fifteen points. The others were near misses. Two darts bounced off the picture on the wall.

'The old fool's aiming at those naked cherubs,' crowed H.H. 'Go on, Simon, see if you can win a free drink for me.'

Simon did his best, but scored a meagre thirty points.

'Idiot!' cried H.H. 'And you always said you were a good darts player.'

'Out of practice,' Simon mumbled.

Meanwhile, someone had opened up the old radiogram and placed a record on the turntable. The cheeky voice of Maurice Chevalier filled the room:

All I want is just one girl,
But I have to have one girl
All I want is one
For a start!

The evening was livening up. Suresh Mathur scored a few points, but it was Krishan who hit the bullseye and claimed a drink on the house.

'Not until I've had my turn,' shouted H.H., and made a grab for the darts.

She flung them at the board at random, missing wildly—so much so that one dart lodged itself in Colonel Wilkie's old felt hat which was hanging from a peg, while another streaked across the room and narrowly missed the Roman nose of Reggie Bhowmik, ex-actor, who had just entered the room accompanied by his demure little wife.

Between ex-actor Reggie and former cricketer Krishan there was no love lost. Both middle aged and no longer in demand, they were rivals in failure. One spoke of the prejudice and incompetence of the cricket selectors, the other of jealousy in the film industry and his subsequent neglect. Both lived in the past—Krishan recalling the one outstanding innings he had played for the country (before being dropped after a series of failures), Reggie living on memories of his one great romantic role before a sagging waistline and alcohol-coarsened features had led to a rapid decline in his popularity. Somehow they had drifted into the backwater that was Dehra in 1950.

There are some places, no matter how dull or lacking in opportunity, which nevertheless take a grip on the individual, especially the more easy-going types, and hold them in thrall, rendering them unfit for life in a larger, more competitive milieu. Dehra was one such place.

The bar at Green's Hotel was their refuge and their strength. Here they could reminisce, hark back to glory days, even speak optimistically of the future. Colonel Wilkie, Suresh Mathur, Krishan Kapoor, Reggie Bhowmik, H.H.—the Maharani—and Simon Lee, were all dropouts, failures in their own way. Had they been busy and successful, they would not have found their way to Green's every evening.

Reggie Bhowmik liked making dramatic entrances, but the Maharani was just as fond of being the centre of attention, and wasn't about to give up centre stage to a fading actor.

'A double whisky for Krishan!' she declared. 'He's the only one here who still has a steady hand.'

'You haven't felt *my* hand,' said Reggie, bearing down on her. 'You missed my nose by a whisker.'

'You'd look better with a scar running down your face,' said H.H. 'Then you might get a role as Frankenstein or the phantom of the opera.'

This touched a raw nerve, as Reggie had been having some difficulty in getting a decent role in recent months. But he snapped back: 'I'll play the phantom on condition that you're cast as the fat soprano—then I shall take great pleasure in strangling you.'

'Let's change the subject,' said his wife Ruby, always ready to pour oil on troubled waters. She moved over to Colonel Wilkie's table and asked: 'How have you been, Colonel?'

'Like an old bus just about moving, and badly in need of spare parts.'

'Well, have a beer with us—and some French fries if we can get any.'

'Cook's on strike,' said Krishan. 'Only liquid diet today.' I saw my opportunity, and piped up again from behind the potted palm. 'I can boil some eggs for you if you like!' There was a stunned silence, broken by Suresh Mathur who said, sounding a little incredulous, 'Young Master Copperfield can boil an egg!'

Everyone clapped, and Krishan said, 'Copperfield has certainly saved the day for us. First he produces a dartboard, and now he's about to save us from starvation. Go to it, Copperfield!'

Off I went, then, not to boil eggs—there weren't any in the kitchen—but to find Sitaram, the room-boy, who was the only person of my age in the hotel. I found him in my room, listening to 'Binaca Geetmala', the popular musical request programme, on my radio.

'We need some eggs,' I told him. 'Boiled.'

'Egg-man comes tomorrow,' he said. 'Cook finished the rest. Made himself an omelette, got drunk, and took off!'

'Well, let's go down to the bazaar and buy some eggs. I've got enough money on me.'

So off we went, and near the clock tower found a street vendor selling boiled eggs. We bought a dozen and hurried back to the bar-room, where Krishan and Reggie were having a heated argument on the relative merits of cricket and football. Reggie didn't think much of cricket, and Krishan didn't think much of football.

'And what's *your* favourite game?' asked Ruby of Suresh Mathur.

'Snakes and ladders,' he said, chuckling, and returned to his drink.

'Boiled eggs!' I announced. 'On the house!'

Sitaram produced saucers, and distributed the eggs among the guests—two each, exactly.

'Do I have to peel my own egg?' asked the Maharani querulously, staring down at the two eggs rolling about on her plate. 'Peel them for me, Simon!'

Simon dutifully cracked one of the eggs and began peeling it for her. 'Not that way, you fool. You're leaving all the skin on it.' And seizing the half-peeled egg from her companion, she flung it across the room, narrowly missing the bartender.

'Good throw!' exclaimed Krishan. 'You'd be great fielding on the boundary.'

'Better at baseball,' said Reggie.

'Snakes and ladders,' said Suresh again, now quite drunk.

Colonel Wilkie, equally drunk, gave a loud belch.

The Maharani got up to leave. 'Well, I'm not going to sit here to be insulted by everyone. Come on, Simon, drive me home!' And she started marching out of the room with an attempt at majesty, but tripped over the hotel cat, an ugly, striped creature who had sensed that there was food around and had come looking for it. The cat caterwauled, H.H. screamed and cursed, Reggie cheered, and Suresh Mather pronounced, 'When two cats are fighting, they make a hideous sound.'

Not to be outdone in nastiness, the Maharani went up to Suresh, looked him up and down, and said, 'It's easy to tell you're a single man.'

'I'm not homosexual,' said Suresh defensively. (The word 'gay' had yet to be used in any sense other than 'happy' in those days.)

'No,' the Maharani smiled wickedly. 'You're single because you are so damn ugly!'

And on that triumphant note she left the room, followed by the obedient Simon.

'Pay no attention to her, Suresh,' said Krishan generously. 'You're better-looking than that old lapdog who follows her around.'

'I understand she's leaving him her fortunes,' said Reggie. 'I could do with some of it myself. Perhaps I could interest her in producing a film.'

'She's tight-fisted,' said Krishan. 'If you look closely at Simon, you'll notice he's wearing the late Maharaja's smoking jacket and deerstalker cap. The old Maharaja loved dressing up like Sherlock Holmes.'

Colonel Wilkie came out of his reverie. 'When I was in Jamnagar—' he began.

'We've heard that a hundred times,' said Krishan.

'*I* haven't,' said Ruby.

'When I was in Jamnagar,' continued Colonel Wilkie, 'I saw Duleep Singh-ji make a hundred. That was against Lord Tennyson's team.'

'Yesterday you said Ranjit Singh-ji,' remarked Krishan.

'I'm not that old,' said Colonel Wilkie, struggling to his feet. 'But old enough to want to go to bed. I'll toddle off now.' Locating his walking-stick, he found his way to the door, wishing everyone goodnight as he passed them. They heard the tap of his walking stick as he walked away down the corridor.

'Shouldn't someone go with him?' asked Ruby. 'It's very late and he isn't too steady on his feet.'

'Oh, he'll find his way home,' said Suresh nonchalantly. 'Lives just around the corner, in rented rooms near the Club.'

'Why doesn't he join the Club?'

'Can't afford it. Neither can I.'

'Neither can I,' said Krishan.

'Neither can we,' added Ruby, sadly. 'And anyway, it's more homely here. Even when the Maharani is around.'

'*She* can afford the Club,' said Suresh. 'But they won't let her in. Created a disturbance once too often. Insulted the secretary and emptied a dish of chicken biryani on his head.'

'Not done,' said Krishan. 'Not cricket.'

'I don't believe it,' said Reggie. 'Can't be true.'

'Calling me a liar?' asked Suresh, bristling.

Ruby poured oil on troubled waters again. 'Interesting if true,' she said. 'And if not true, still interesting.'

'Mark Twain.'

My mother came along the corridor just as Krishan had shown off his knowledge of literature, and found me behind the palms listening to all this fascinating talk.

'Time you went to your room, young man,' she said.

'I'm waiting for everyone to go home,' I said. 'Then I'll help Sitaram tidy up. There's no cook, as you know.'

'Let him stay,' called Suresh from his bar stool. 'It's all part of his education. And he's old enough for a glass of beer. How old are you, sonny?'

'Sixteen,' I said.

'Well, enjoy yourself. It's later than you think.'

But I wasn't thinking of beer just then. I knew there were sausages in the fridge, and I had every intention of polishing them off as soon as all the guests had gone. I wanted to be a writer, but I had no intention of starving in a garret. However, all thoughts of food vanished when I looked across the room and saw Colonel Wilkie framed in the opposite doorway. He was staring at us through the glass. The glass door then opened of its own volition, and Colonel Wilkie stepped into the room.

We all looked up, and Reggie said, 'Back again, Colonel? Still feeling thirsty?' But Colonel Wilkie ignored the jibe, and walked slowly across the room to the table where he had been sitting. This was close to where I was standing. He bent down and picked up his pipe from the table. He'd forgotten it when he'd left the bar-room. Shoving the pipe into his pocket, he turned and retraced his steps, leaving the room by the door from which he had entered.

'Well, I'm blowed,' said Krishan. 'I thought he was sleepwalking.'

'Never goes anywhere without his pipe,' said Suresh. 'A perfect example of single-mindedness.'

'Didn't say a word.'

'The pipe was all that mattered.'

'Like a favourite cricket bat,' said Krishan.

'Maybe I'll come back for mine when I'm dead.'

A silence fell upon the room. The mention of death had a sobering effect upon the small group. And come to think of it, Colonel Wilkie on his return to the bar-room had something of the zombie about him—the walking dead.

There was a commotion in the passageway, and my mother burst into the room, followed by the night-watchman.

'Colonel Wilkie's dead,' said my mother. 'He collapsed on his steps about half an hour ago.'

'But he was here five minutes ago,' said Krishan.

'No, sir,' said Gopal the watchman. 'I went home with him when he left here some time back. Madam said to keep an eye on him. When we got to his place, he began climbing his steps with some difficulty. I helped him to the top step, and then he collapsed. I dragged him into his room and then ran for Dr Bhist. He is there now.'

There was silence for a couple of minutes, and then Ruby

said, 'We all saw him. Colonel Wilkie.'

'We saw his ghost,' Krishan murmured.

'He came for his pipe,' said Suresh quietly. 'I told you he wouldn't go anywhere without it.'

Colonel Wilkie was buried the next day, and we made sure his pipe was buried with him. We did not want him turning up from time to time, looking for it. It could be a bit unnerving for the customers.

In all the excitement I'd forgotten about the sausages, but decided they would keep until after the funeral.

All the regular barflies turned up for the funeral. H.H. was quite sloshed when she arrived and had to be extricated from an open grave into which she had slipped, the ground being soft and yielding after recent rain. She blamed secretary Simon for the mishap and called him an 'ullu ka patha'—son of an owl—but he was quite used to such broadsides and took them in his stride. Was it love or loyalty or dependence that kept him in abeyance? Or was it, as some said, the prospect of becoming her heir? If so, he was paying a heavy price well in advance of such a prospect. Not everyone relishes being abused and kicked around in public by a half-crazed maharani.

When Colonel Wilkie's coffin was lowered into the grave, we all said 'Cheers!' He would have liked that. We then returned to Green's for an early opening of the bar. Alcoholics Unanimous held a subdued but not too melancholy meeting.

But bad news was in store for everyone. A day or two later, I heard the owner, our Sardar-ji, inform my mother that the hotel had been sold and that she'd have to leave at the end of the month. She'd been expecting something like this, and had already accepted a matron's job at one of the schools in the valley. As for me, I was to be packed off to England to my aunt's home in Jersey. The prospect did not thrill me, but

I was more or less resigned to it. And there did not appear to be much future for me in Dehra.

Even before the month was out, workers had begun pulling down parts of the building. It was to be rebuilt as a cinema hall, and would show the latest hits from Bombay. It was even rumoured that Dilip Kumar, the biggest star of that era, would inaugurate the new cinema when it was ready to open.

The spirit and character of a building lasts only while the building lasts. Remove the roof-beams, pull down the walls, smash the stairways, and you are left with nothing but memories. Even the ghosts have nowhere to go.

An old hotel that once had a personality of its own was now dismantled with startling rapidity. It had gone up slowly, brick by brick; it came down like a house of cards. No treasures cascaded from its walls; no skeletons were discovered. In two or three days the demolishers had wiped out the past, removed Green's Hotel from the face of the earth so effectively that it might never have existed.

Searching through the ruins one day, I found a bottle-opener lying in the dust, and kept it as a souvenir.

The bar had been the only common factor in the lives of those disparate individuals who had come there so regularly—drawn to the place rather than to each other.

Now they went their different ways—Suresh Mathur to the Club, the Maharani to her card table and private bar, Krishan to a public school as a cricket coach, Reggie Bhowmik and Ruby to Darjeeling to make a documentary... Sitaram continued to work for my mother, so I had his company whenever he was free.

The cinema came up quite rapidly, but I had left for England before it opened. When I returned five years later, it was showing Madhubala and Guru Dutt in a romantic comedy, *Mr & Mrs 55*.

Then I moved to Delhi.

In recent years, some of the old single cinemas have been closing down, giving way to multiplexes. The other day, passing through Dehra, I saw that 'our' cinema hall was being pulled down. 'What now?' I asked my taxi driver. 'A multiplex?'

'No, sir. A shopping mall!'

And such is progress.

I think I'm the only one around who is old enough to remember the old Green's Hotel, its dusty corridors, shabby bar-room, and oddball customers. All have gone. All forgotten! Not even footprints in the sands of time. But by putting down this memoir of an evening or two at that forgotten watering place, I think I have cheated Time just a little.

SOME HILL STATION GHOSTS

Shimla has its phantom-rickshaw and Lansdowne its headless horseman. Mussoorie has its woman in white. Late at night, she can be seen sitting on the parapet wall on the winding road up to the hill station. Don't stop to offer her a lift. She will fix you with her evil eye and ruin your holiday.

The Mussoorie taxi drivers and other locals call her Bhoot Aunty. Everyone has seen her at some time or the other. To give her a lift is to court disaster. Many accidents have been attributed to her baleful presence. And when people pick themselves up from the road (or are picked up by concerned citizens), Bhoot Aunty is nowhere to be seen, although survivors swear that she was in the car with them.

Ganesh Saili, Abha and I were coming back from Dehradun late one night when we saw this woman in white sitting on the parapet by the side of the road. As our headlights fell on her, she turned her face away, Ganesh, being a thorough gentleman, slowed down and offered her a lift. She turned towards us then, and smiled a wicked smile. She seemed quite attractive except that her canines protruded slightly in vampire fashion.

'Don't stop!' screamed Abha. 'Don't even look at her! It's Aunty!'

Ganesh pressed down on the accelerator and sped past her. Next day, we heard that a tourist's car had gone off the road and the occupants had been severely injured. The accident had taken place shortly after they had stopped to pick up a woman in white who had wanted a lift. But she was not among the injured.

◾

Miss Ripley-Bean, an old English lady who was my neighbour when I lived near Wynberg-Allen school, told me that her family was haunted by a malignant phantom head that always appeared before the death of one of her relatives.

She said her brother saw this apparition the night before her mother died, and both she and her sister saw it before the death of their father. The sister slept in the same room. They were both awakened one night by a curious noise in the cupboard facing their beds. One of them began getting out of bed to see if their cat was in the room, when the cupboard door suddenly opened and a luminous head appeared. It was covered with matted hair and appeared to be in an advanced stage of decomposition. Its fleshless mouth grinned at the terrified sisters. And then, as they crossed themselves, it vanished. The next day they learnt that their father, who was in Lucknow, had died suddenly, at about the time that they had seen the death's head.

◾

Everyone likes to hear stories about haunted houses; even sceptics will listen to a ghost story, while casting doubts on its veracity.

Rudyard Kipling wrote a number of memorable ghost stories set in India—*Imray's Return, The Phantom Rickshaw, The Mark of the Beast, The End of the Passage*—his favourite milieu being the haunted dak bungalow. But it was only after his return to England that he found himself actually having to live in a haunted house. He wrote about it in his autobiography, *Something of Myself.*

The spring of '96 saw us in Torquay, where we found a house for our heads that seemed almost too good to be true. It was large and bright, with big rooms each and all open to the sun, the ground embellished with great trees and the warm land dipping southerly to the clean sea under the Mary Church cliffs. It had been inhabited for thirty years by three old maids.

The revelation came in the shape of a growing depression which enveloped us both—a gathering blackness of mind and sorrow of the heart, that each put down to the new, soft climate and, without telling the other, fought against for long weeks. It was the Feng-shui—the Spirit of the house itself—that darkened the sunshine and fell upon us every time we entered, checking the very words on our lips... We paid forfeit and fled. More than thirty years later we returned down the steep little road to that house, and found, quite unchanged, the same brooding spirit of deep despondency within the rooms.

Again, thirty years later, he returned to this house in his short story, 'The House Surgeon', in which two sisters cannot come to terms with the suicide of a third sister, and brood upon the tragedy day and night until their thoughts saturate every room of the house.

Many years ago, I had a similar experience in a house in Dehradun, in which an elderly English couple had died from neglect and starvation. In 1947, when many European residents were leaving the town and emigrating to the UK, this poverty-stricken old couple, sick and friendless, had been forgotten. Too ill to go out for food or medicine, they had died in their beds, where they were discovered several days later by the landlord's munshi.

The house stood empty for several years. No one wanted to live in it. As a young man, I would sometimes roam about the neglected grounds or explore the cold, bare rooms, now stripped of furniture, doorless and windowless, and I would be assailed by a feeling of deep gloom and depression. Of course I knew what had happened there, and that may have contributed to the effect the place had on me. But when I took a friend, Jai Shankar, through the house, he told me he felt quite sick with apprehension and fear. 'Ruskin, why have you brought me to this awful house?' he said. 'I'm sure it's haunted.' And only then did I tell him about the tragedy that had taken place within its walls.

Today, the house is used as a government office. No one lives in it at night except for a Gurkha chowkidar, a man of strong nerves who sleeps in the back verandah. The atmosphere of the place doesn't bother him, but he does hear strange sounds in the night. 'Like someone crawling about on the floor above,' he tells me. 'And someone groaning. These old houses are noisy places...'

◆

A morgue is not a noisy place, as a rule. And for a morgue attendant, corpses are silent companions.

Old Mr Jacob, who lives just behind my cottage, was once a morgue attendant for the local mission hospital. In those days it was situated at Sunny Bank, about a hundred metres up the hill from here. One of the outhouses served as the morgue: Mr Jacob begs me not to identify it.

He tells me of a terrifying experience he went through when he was doing night duty at the morgue.

'The body of a young man was found floating in the Aglar River, behind Landour, and was brought to the morgue while I was on night duty. It was placed on the table and covered with a sheet.

'I was quite accustomed to seeing corpses of various kinds and did not mind sharing the same room with them, even after dark. On this occasion a friend had promised to join me, and to pass the time I strolled around the room, whistling a popular tune. I think it was "Danny Boy", if I remember right. My friend was a long time coming, and I soon got tired of whistling and sat down on the bench beside the table. The night was very still, and I began to feel uneasy. My thoughts went to the boy who had drowned and I wondered what he had been like when he was alive. Dead bodies are so impersonal...

'The morgue had no electricity, just a kerosene lamp, and after some time I noticed that the flame was very low. As I was about to turn it up, it suddenly went out. I lit the lamp again, after extending the wick. I returned to the bench, but I had not been sitting there for long when the lamp again went out, and something moved very softly and quietly past me.

'I felt quite sick and faint, and could hear my heart pounding away. The strength had gone out of my legs, otherwise I would have fled from the room. I felt quite weak and helpless, unable even to call out.

'Presently the footsteps came nearer and nearer. Something cold and icy touched one of my hands and felt its way up towards my neck and throat. It was behind me, then it was before me. Then it was *over* me. I was in the arms of the corpse!

'I must have fainted, because when I woke up I was on the floor, and my friend was trying to revive me. The corpse was back on the table.'

'It may have been a nightmare,' I suggested. 'Or you allowed your imagination to run riot.'

'No,' said Mr Jacobs. 'There were wet, slimy marks on my clothes. And the feet of the corpse matched the wet footprints on the floor.'

After this experience, Mr Jacobs refused to do any more night duty at the morgue.

♦

From Herbertpur near Paonta you can go up to Kalsi, and then up the hill road to Chakrata.

Chakrata is in a security zone, most of it off limits to tourists, which is one reason why it has remained unchanged in 150 years of its existence. This small town's population of 1,500 is the same today as it was in 1947—probably the only town in India that hasn't shown a population increase.

Courtesy a government official, I was fortunate enough to be able to stay in the forest rest house on the outskirts of the town. This is a new building, the old rest house—a little way downhill—having fallen into disuse. The chowkidar told me the old rest house was haunted, and that this was the real reason for its having been abandoned. I was a bit sceptical about this, and asked him what kind of haunting took place in it. He told me that he had himself gone through a frightening experience in the old house, when he had gone there to light a fire for some forest officers who were expected that night. After lighting the fire, he looked round and saw a large black animal, like a wild cat, sitting on the wooden floor and gazing into the fire. 'I called out to it, thinking it was someone's pet. The creature turned, and looked full at me with eyes that were human, and a face that was the face of an ugly woman. The creature snarled at me, and the snarl became an angry howl. Then it vanished!'

'And what did you do?' I asked.

'I vanished too,' said the chowkidar. 'I haven't been down to that house again.'

I did not volunteer to sleep in the old house but made myself comfortable in the new one, where I hoped I would not be troubled by any phantom. However, a large rat kept me company, gnawing away at the woodwork of a chest of drawers. Whenever I switched on the light it would be silent, but as soon as the light was off, it would start gnawing away again.

This reminded me of a story old Miss Kellner (of my Dehra childhood) told me, of a young man who was desperately in love with a girl who did not care for him. One day, when he was following her in the street, she turned on him and, pointing to a rat which some boys had just killed, said, 'I'd as soon marry that rat as marry you.' He took her cruel words so much to heart that he pined away and died. After his death the girl was haunted at night by a rat and occasionally she would be bitten. When the family decided to emigrate, they travelled down to Bombay in order to embark on a ship sailing for London. The ship had just left the quay, when shouts and screams were heard from the pier. The crowd scattered, and a huge rat with fiery eyes ran down to the end of the quay. It sat there, screaming with rage, then jumped into the water and disappeared. After that (according to Miss Kellner), the girl was not haunted again.

Old dak bungalows and forest rest houses have a reputation for being haunted. And most hill stations have their resident ghosts—and ghost writers! But I will not extend this catalogue of ghostly hauntings and visitations, as I do not want to discourage tourists from visiting Landour and Mussoorie. In some countries, ghosts are an added attraction for tourists. Britain boasts of hundreds of haunted castles and stately homes, and visitors to Romania seek out Transylvania and Dracula's castle. So do we promote Bhoot Aunty as a tourist attraction? Only if she reforms and stops sending vehicles off those hairpin bends that lead to Mussoorie.

BORN EVIL

'Can someone be born evil?' asked Mr Lobo, handing Miss Ripley-Bean a glass of nimbu paani as they sat on the sunny verandah lounge of the Royal. 'Be totally evil, that is—from birth through manhood and into old age. Someone without a conscience, someone who inflicts cruelty without a qualm, who cares a damn for what the world would think of him. Someone like Hitler, perhaps?'

'Hitler was vegetarian,' said Miss Ripley-Bean, helping herself to a cracker and giving it to her Tibetan terrier, Fluff, who gobbled it up. A notice in the hotel lobby said 'No dogs allowed', but this was blissfully ignored by Miss Ripley-Bean. After all, Fluff was no ordinary dog.

'What has that to do with it?' asked Mr Lobo, curious. 'Being a vegetarian?'

'Well, presumably he was kind to animals. Didn't approve of killing and eating them. But of course he hated Jews—and Russians—and gypsies—and Black people.'

'And killed them without compunction, or had his lackeys do the job for him. He thought that was his duty. Or rather, his policy.'

'And he was driven by hatred. Don't forget that.'

'So would you say he was born evil?'

'I think the evil grew in him,' said Miss Ripley-Bean, giving Fluff another cracker. The plate of crackers would soon be empty.

Neither Miss Ripley-Bean nor Mr Lobo were hotel guests. Miss Ripley-Bean's father had sold the hotel to Nandu's father at the time of Independence, on condition that she, May Ripley-Bean, could continue to live there for the rest of her days. He had died shortly afterwards. And Mr Lobo was the hotel pianist. He had been there for a couple of years. Every evening he would sit at the piano in the lounge, strumming out old favourites or popular film tunes for the benefit of a dwindling clientele. In the late 1960s hill stations were going through a slump, and classier hotels like the Royal were feeling the pinch.

Miss Ripley-Bean and Mr Lobo had struck up a quaint friendship. She was almost seventy and he was just forty. Neither had ever been married. Mr Lobo enjoyed listening to Miss Ripley-Bean's tales of old Mussoorie and the Doon valley, and she enjoyed listening to him play Viennese waltzes and romantic ballads from old movies. Miss Ripley-Bean had been quite a movie buff once—a fan of Eddie Cantor, Al Jolson, Fred Astaire, Nelson Eddy and, of course, Greta Garbo, but that had been back in the thirties and forties, when the cinemas had been flooded with Hollywood's best. But over the years her eyesight had deteriorated, and now, unless she sat in the front row with the rickshaw boys and shop assistants, she couldn't see very much. Also, she couldn't take Fluff into a cinema hall; he might want to pee on people's legs.

'I have never known anyone who was completely evil,' said Mr Lobo reflectively. 'Even Hitler had his softer side. He could love Eva Braun—and die beside her. Have you known anyone who was completely evil? Born evil—evil to the end of his days?'

'Evil is an aberration of personality, often ingrained in the mind at birth,' said Miss Ripley-Bean.

'You mean it's in the genes—it can't be helped?'

'I am not sure. I knew a couple who were both very good people. And yet they had a son who took to crime like a duck to water.'

'It could go far back, to earlier forebears—that propensity for crime.'

'Quite possibly. You see, this young man—or rather boy, as he was when I knew him—had the most charming and innocent-looking face that you could imagine. It was almost angelic. Everyone fell for him—old ladies, young women, strict headmasters, peppery old colonels, older boys, younger boys, schoolgirls. And he smiled at everyone and was oh-so-polite and well mannered. But he hated all of them—he hated everyone!'

'But why—was there any reason for it?'

'None at all. He was just made that way. The rest of humanity meant absolutely nothing to him. They were just his playthings, his toys. He played with them and then threw them away. But not before damaging them a little—sometimes more than a little.'

'And who was this paragon of evil? You seem to have known him well.'

Miss Ripley-Bean gave Fluff another cracker. 'Young Alexander. Yes, I knew him. But I did not really know him. No one did. In a way he lived in a world of his own making—he made things happen. Like dropping a lighted match in the petrol tank of a motorcycle and watching it go up in flames. Or firing Diwali rockets through the open window of the headmaster's bedroom and destroying all the bed linen.'

'He must have been crackers,' said Mr Lobo.

'Yes, but not this sort of cracker'——and Miss Ripley-Bean slipped another Royal cracker to Fluff, who accepted graciously. 'He was cracked in the head all right, but in an evil way—like Emperor Nero, who loved to watch his slaves being torn apart by lions. It was fire that excited Alexander. Conflagrations! If he heard that there was a building on fire, in Mussoorie or Dehradun or wherever his family happened to be staying, he'd rush to watch. Sometimes he'd pretend to help the firefighters, get involved in what was happening, but it was the spreading fire that he really enjoyed—and the screams of people who were trapped inside or running about on the roof or jumping from windows.

'There was this big fire at Green's Hotel back in the late forties. The ballroom went up in flames. Alexander was just a boy then, home from school; his family lived in one wing of the hotel. Out front was a ballroom that had come up during the war. American and British soldiers would come over in the evenings—Dehra was a recreation centre for Allied soldiers—and dance with the Anglo-Indian girls. They were great dancers, those girls, and so pretty. Fights broke out over them. Of course, the Americans had more money to spend and that was part of the trouble.

'Alexander was fourteen at the time, too young to be familiar with that lot, but he liked listening to the band—Jimmy Cotton and his Band, they came from the Imperial in Delhi, just to play at Green's.

'No one knows how the fire started. And no one believed Alexander had anything to do with it—he looked so charming, so cute, just sitting there behind the band, his eyes sparkling with excitement as he tapped his feet to a tango or swayed to the rhythms of a rumba. The air was full of cigarette smoke, so at first no one noticed the smoke rising from an alcove near the bar. Had someone thrown a lighted cigarette on to a rug? Very careless but common enough at these dance parties. Rugs were always being ruined, Only this time the rug was already soaked in kerosene—a spill from an oil lamp, probably—and in no time at all the rug caught fire and the ballroom was full of smoke.

'"Fire! Fire!" It was Alexander shouting.

'And sure enough, the curtains were on fire, and the dancing stopped and the band stopped playing. Yes, the dancing had stopped, but now Alexander was dancing, doing a tap dance of his own, as he grew more and more excited.

'There was panic in the ballroom. Girls, soldiers, musicians, waiters, everyone rushed for the exit. There was only one exit, and in the melee two of the girls fell to the ground and were crushed to death. By the time a fire engine arrived, the flames were out of control. Young Alexander made a big show of helping the firefighters—giving instructions, directing the water hoses, dashing about with a fire extinguisher—oh, he was quite the hero. Later, everyone commended him for his efforts. It was all an act of course. No one had any idea that he was the real culprit.'

'Diabolical,' said Mr Lobo.

'Exactly. The face of an angel and the mind of the devil. You know, the world is full of criminals and many end up behind bars so that society is protected from them. But they are, for the most part, ordinary people—people like you and me—who have transgressed, crossed the line of decency, given in to their animal instincts or succumbed to human greed and paid the price for it. But Alexander was consistently evil. He went from one brazen act of evil to another—and got away with it, time after time.'

'What happened next?'

'There were minor incidents—a fire in a cinema, at a railway station—but these were detected in time and brought under control. Alexander's school gymnasium burnt down quite mysteriously. He was sixteen when he set fire to his parents' house. This was down in Rajpur, where they lived at the time. It was a lovely old mansion, so big that Alexander's parents were able to use part of it as a guest house. But the guests did not stay very long—not with Alexander around. He would introduce snakes into their rooms, or monitor lizards, or stink bombs that he made himself. The paying guests were happy to pay their bills and go elsewhere. He would even torment his little sister. One day, while she was asleep, he cut most of her hair off, leaving just shreds and patches. He was well thrashed for this by his father.

'Vengeful by nature, he waited until they had all gone out to a Sunday church service. Then he sent the cook and the gardener out on errands and set about making a pile of all the best furniture in the front room before setting it alight.

'"I am Guy Fawkes today," he declared, addressing an invisible audience. Guy Fawkes, who had once tried to burn down the English Parliament, was his history-book hero.

'The furniture made a great bonfire. It spread from the sofas and tables to the costly rugs that his mother had collected and then to the curtains, and then from room to room, upstairs and downstairs, rapidly spreading through the entire house.

'The cook returned from his errand to find his kitchen ablaze, and flames leaping from the bedroom windows. Was the Baba safe? He was a good man and feared for the safety of the errant youth. He could not believe that it was Alexander who had started it all. He dashed about, calling out to the Baba, the name by which Alexander was known to the servants. Presently Alexander emerged from a wing of the house, covered in soot.

'"House on fire," he said calmly. "Better call the fire brigade."

'But there was no fire brigade in Rajpur. And there was not much that the cook and the gardener and the helpful neighbours could do with buckets of water. When Alexander's parents and sister returned from church, they were confronted by the smoking ruin of their old home. And their pet Alsatian had disappeared in the flames.'

Mr Lobo poured out another glass of nimbu paani for Miss Ripley-Bean, and she in turn gave Fluff another cracker.

'So what happened to Alexander? Did they send him to a reform home?'

'Oh no, they doted on him and wouldn't accept that he was responsible for it, although in the back of their minds they must have known that he was the devil incarnate. We can never believe the worst of our own progeny, can we?'

'I wouldn't know,' said Mr Lobo, a confirmed bachelor.

'Nor would I, really,' said Miss Ripley-Bean. 'But over the years I've seen it in so many people who rush to the defence of their beloved Tom, Dev or Danny, in spite of their having committed the most heinous of crimes. So Alexander's parents covered up for their diabolic boy even though it was their own house he'd burnt down!

'Well, he couldn't go to college. He'd already been expelled from two schools. So they sent him to a Bible school in Landour, run by a couple of homely American missionaries. Poor boy, they said, he has had a bad time of it—misunderstood by his parents and teachers; we'll put him in the Lord's way and, who knows, one day he might make a good preacher! And they put him in charge of the community library.'

'That should have cured him.'

'Hardly. Books! All those books. Such a temptation to the little firebug. What could make a better fire? Books burn so well—and who needs them anyway, or so reasons Alexander, who values everything on the basis of inflammability. Some of the world's greatest libraries have been lost to fires, or so he's heard, so why not add this little one to the list? Most of them are religious books anyway, and no one bothers to read them. The ragman buys up the old ones and turns them into paper bags.

'So there is quite a conflagration, and although the students of the nearby Pinewood School turn out in force, with buckets and jerrycans of water, they can do nothing to put out the fire. And meanwhile, Alexander is sitting on the hillside singing an old sea-shanty that he'd learnt in his nursery days:

> *Fire in the galley, fire down below,*
> *Fetch a bucket of water, boys,*
> *There's fire down below.*
> *Fire up aloft, and fire down below,*
> *Fetch a bucket of water, boys,*
> *There's fire down below.*

'He'd also heard the good missionary lady speak of this wicked old world being consumed by "fire and brimstone", and he felt that this was a good beginning.

'Once again, no blame attached to Alexander. It was a short circuit, obviously. Or a careless smoker. And Alexander did not smoke.

'But with the library gone, some other occupation had to be found for him. And since he was the outdoor type, why not appoint him as assistant to the estate manager of Pinewood School, Mr Rajan, who was due for retirement in a few months? The missionaries were directors of the school and could easily arrange things. The estate was extensive, taking in the entire hillside and a large tract of pine forest. Mr Rajan had a hard time keeping away the villagers who would slip in at night to cut branches for firewood. He needed help.

'And Alexander turned out to be a handy helper. He kept the villagers away by strutting about with a loaded rifle, occasionally firing it at random. In the autumn, pine needles covered the ground, and by December the pine cones were falling.

'The school people used the pine cones in their fireplaces, and Alexander kept them well supplied. He had also discovered that pine cones burn beautifully. School was about to close for winter when a fire broke out in the forest. It hadn't rained for weeks, the grass had turned yellow, the pine needles dry and brittle, and Alexander had made a little bonfire of cones just for his private amusement, and he couldn't resist watching it spread.

'A boy stuck his head out of a dormitory window and exclaimed, "Look! There are flames in the forest!" And soon, everyone was running around, eager to see the forest fire and speculating on whether or not it would reach the school building.

'The village was actually more in danger than the school, for the trees were close to the fields. But a strong wind carried the flames towards the school, burning leaves and floating embers leaping from one tree to another, while the grass beneath was a carpet of fire. A flock of sheep, returning to the village, perished in the smoke and flames. Their attendants, two youngsters, were lucky to escape. The school servants and some of the bigger boys ran about with buckets of sand or water. Several pine martens and a barking deer fled the forest in panic, as did a party of flying squirrels and several large brown owls.

'Alexander was very prominent in all this activity, at times directing the firefighters and at times running about wildly and without any clear sense of purpose. Standing on a cliff edge and waving his arms to a crowd of spectators, he slipped on the pine needles and went tumbling down the steep slope into the burning undergrowth. His clothes on fire, he ran here and there screaming for help, but he was overcome by the smoke and flames and vanished from sight.

'Eventually the wind shifted and the fire burnt itself out. Mr Rajan and his helpers went in search of Alexander and found his charred body at the edge of the forest.'

'So all things wicked must come to an end,' commented Mr Lobo. 'It's all a matter of time. And time must pass...'

'Time has nothing else to do, except pass,' said Miss Ripley-Bean wryly. 'And as for Alexander, he was accounted a hero and, being dead, he could not change his status to that of villain. They gave him a grand funeral and a headstone with an inscription that mentioned his bravery in helping to prevent a forest fire from enveloping the school. His grave is up there in the Landour cemetery.'

Miss Ripley-Bean gave Fluff the last of the crackers and rose to go. 'Time for my afternoon nap,' she said. 'It's always nice to talk to you, Mr Lobo.'

That evening Mr Lobo went for a long walk, which took him to the Landour cemetery. After wandering around for some time, he found Alexander's tombstone. As he returned to the hotel, the sun fell away to the west, which now reddened to receive it. He looked very thoughtful as he tapped on Miss Ripley-Bean's front door.

He found the old lady sipping a crème de menthe. She made her own liqueur and treated herself to a couple of glasses every evening.

'Have some crème de menthe, Mr Lobo. There is nothing else, I'm afraid,' she said by way of greeting.

'No, thanks,' said Mr Lobo, who hated crème de menthe. 'I won't stay. Just wanted to tell you that I visited the Landour cemetery.'

'And did you find the grave?'

'Yes, I did. It was quite clearly inscribed. But it gave his full name. John Alexander Bean. Is that correct?'

'Yes, that was his name,' said Miss Ripley Bean. 'He was my brother.'

THE DARYAGANJ STRANGLER

Summertime. The hotel was full, the mall road crowded. Mussoorie was enjoying its annual invasion of holiday makers, eager to escape the heat and dust of the cities of the plains. The hill station thrived on its visitors; and the visitors thrived on the clear sky and bracing air of the Himalayan foothills.

Miss Ripley-Bean and Mr Lobo were enjoying a mid-morning coffee break in the shade of the huge deodar that had been planted in front of the Royal Hotel when it had opened just over a hundred years ago. The late Mr Ripley-Bean had been one of its founders, and his daughter, an elderly spinster, was the legal occupant of two small rooms in a corner of the tennis court block. She was now seventy, but 'full of beans' according to everyone who knew her. Mr Lobo, the hotel pianist and sometimes assistant manager (whenever managers were on leave, which happened frequently), enjoyed the old lady's company, even though he was almost half her age. She reminded him of a favourite aunt in Goa.

This balmy summer morning they were discussing the activities of the Daryaganj strangler.

Daryaganj was a historic area of Delhi, part commercial, part residential, linking New Delhi to the old city. In the times of the Mughals it had been known for its elegant villas, with their views of the winding Yamuna River. Now it was an overcrowded locality, a clutter of shops, offices, homes and vehicles ranging from cars to motorcycles to handcarts.

'This serial killer,' said Miss Ripley-Bean, 'why does he operate in this particular area—why not Paharganj or Jor Bagh?'

'I've no idea,' said Mr Lobo. 'Probably lives in Daryaganj. And if he's the sort of killer who likes to prowl around at night, he will probably feel at home on familiar streets.'

'And his victims—what were they like? Did he take anything from them?'

'It seems not. A woman was found strangled in the driver's seat of her car. Her expensive rings and necklace had not been touched. A businessman found on the street outside his office still had a roll of banknotes in his pocket. More than one woman was killed—several men—all the victims quite prosperous, but nothing stolen.'

'Interesting,' said Miss Ripley-Bean, 'And now—at least, according to the papers—there has been a pause in his activities. No victims for over a month.'

'Perhaps he's dead. Or taking a break. On holiday, like everyone else,' ventured Mr Lobo.

'Well, let's hope he doesn't come to Mussoorie for his holiday. Or stay at the Royal,' said Miss Ripley-Bean. 'We are quite full, aren't we?'

'Almost,' said Mr Lobo with a grin. 'Except for that room just next to yours. The haunted room.'

It was Miss Ripley-Bean's turn to smile. 'I make sure it's haunted, you know. Just to ensure I don't get a noisy neighbour. And it does give me the shivers whenever I look through the window. I keep seeing that poor man hanging there— Mr Manohar—the manager who hanged himself. It seems he was in debt all over the place, and falsifying the hotel accounts.'

Here there was a distraction. Fluff, Miss Ripley-Bean's Tibetan terrier, emerged from beneath a bench, barking furiously, and set off in hot pursuit of a couple of monkeys that had been trying to get into one of the rooms.

'These monkeys are really too many now,' observed Miss Ripley-Bean. 'Soon they'll be occupying the ballroom and the kitchen. But I'm wondering—this Daryaganj strangler—could he perhaps be among us already, enjoying his holiday? This hotel is packed with people—might he be one of them?'

'What an alarming thought!' said Mr Lobo.

The Daryaganj strangler was indeed taking a break, not because he had lost his appetite for strangling people he disliked, but because his last intended victim, a resourceful editor of a women's magazine, had managed to break two of his fingers before he could get a firm grip on her throat. She had then kicked him in the groin and made her escape—in time to bring out the next issue of *Women's Realm* right on time.

Our strangler now had two of his fingers in splints, having told his doctors that he had jammed them in the door of his car.

Yes, he had a car, a pretty red Ford Fiesta, and he was now driving it up to Mussoorie for a much-needed holiday. The splints had gone, the fingers were healing fast and his palms were itching to be put to use again.

Miss Ripley-Bean was woken from her afternoon siesta by the short inquiring barks of Fluff. Someone had finally occupied the room next door. But it wasn't until late evening that she caught a glimpse of her neighbour. He was a small, wiry man wearing thick-lensed spectacles who peered around him in the gathering gloom, trying to get his bearings. He had a slight limp.

To Miss Ripley-Bean he did not look like someone who could strangle a child, let alone an adult; but then she noticed his hands. They were large, long-fingered hands, almost like a musician's; even Mr Lobo did not have such large hands.

It wasn't until the following morning that Miss Ripley-Bean

met her neighbour. He was sitting on a bench not far from the tennis court block, and he was flipping through the pages of a bound manuscript. Miss Ripley-Bean was returning from a brisk morning walk, Fluff at her heels. The stranger looked up at her approach. She gave him a friendly good morning, and he acknowledged her greeting with a little nod. He did not smile. He was a serious person who seldom smiled.

'You look like a scholar,' observed Miss Ripley-Bean, always curious about people's occupations.

'A novelist,' said the scholar, holding up his manuscript. *'The Great Indian Love Story.'*

The little man on the bench did not look like a great lover, but then, thought Miss Ripley-Bean, you never could tell with men. Sometimes these skinny, undernourished types turned out to be sexual gymnasts! Thoughtfully, she placed herself on a garden seat opposite the newcomer. No one's going to attempt to make love to me, admitted Miss Ripley-Bean to herself, but I don't like the look of those hands—or the way they keep twitching!

'I've always wanted to meet a novelist, but that isn't the same thing, is it?'

'No,' said the novelist, with a look of contempt. 'Do you read novels?'

'Only crime stories,' confessed Miss Ripley-Bean. 'Agatha Christie and Mary Roberts Rinehart.'

'Poor stuff. You ought to read my novel.'

'Well, as soon as it's published, I shall get a copy for myself.'

'Published! But no one will publish it!'

'Why not?'

'It's far too good for them!' The young man was getting agitated. His mouth twitched, the veins stood out on his forehead. 'They don't know anything about writing, the publishers we have today! All they want is soppy love stories or self-improvement books or financial scandals or how to get rich overnight. Money, money, money!'

'Well, I suppose it makes the world go round. Could do with a little myself. Maybe your book will make you rich too!'

'It will, if someone publishes it.'

Miss Ripley-Bean promised to read the manuscript, and the young author looked quite pleased; he was no longer agitated.

'My name is Roshan Puri,' he said. 'You will hear of me one day.'

Miss Ripley-Bean did not see Mr Puri for two or three days. There was a lock on his door and he was still the official occupant, having paid a week's rent in advance. But no one seemed to know where he had gone. This wasn't unusual. Sometimes residents took off for a day or two, visiting Rishikesh or one of the pilgrim destinations higher up in the mountains.

Miss Ripley-Bean read the novel, or tried to read it. It did not make much sense to her. In places it read like Barbara Cartland, in places like Lobsang Rampa, in others like Kahlil Gibran, and she suspected that the writer had lifted large portions of his book from their works. In the novel, the hero has a double, a Hitler-like character who rules the world with an iron fist; but our hero, with a little help from a slave girl, gets rid of the dictator and takes his place, bringing peace and prosperity to all nations. The hero also happens to be the author.

'Not a bad idea,' mused Miss Ripley-Bean, 'except that it's all such a muddle. Mad, quite mad!'

On the third morning of Mr Puri's absence, Mr Lobo walked over with the morning newspaper.

'Has our Nobel Prize candidate returned?' he asked.

'No sign of him,' said Miss Ripley-Bean. 'But he left his

window open, and the monkeys have been in and out.'

'Tearing up his manuscript, no doubt. Well, there's a publisher found dead in Dehradun, just outside the gate of his house. Seems he'd gone out for an after-dinner stroll; he's been strangled with an electrical cord. Could it have been our guest?'

'I hope not. I'd rather the Daryaganj strangler confined his activities to Daryaganj.'

'I hear all the publishers are moving out to Gurgaon. Some of them are keeping dogs!'

'Well, we're not publishers, are we, Fluff?' Miss Ripley-Bean gave Fluff a ginger biscuit, which was consumed with relish.

'Well, take care, Aunty May,' said Mr Lobo, departing. 'And let me know when he gets back.'

Mr Puri turned up at teatime, looking quite spry, refreshed and pleased with himself.

'He looks quite harmless,' thought Miss Ripley-Bean.

Fluff didn't think so. He growled at the approach of their neighbour.

'So did you get a chance to read my book? Don't you think it's a masterpiece?'

Over the years, Miss Ripley-Bean had learnt to be diplomatic with vain young men. They were apt to go off the handle if you made fun of them.

'Most interesting,' she said. 'I couldn't put it down. Here's the manuscript, and I wish you luck with it. But don't leave it lying around; the monkeys are a great nuisance.'

'And so are publishers,' he said quite venomously. 'I believe there's one staying in the hotel.'

'Not that I know of,' said Miss Ripley-Bean. 'But then I wouldn't know. I'm not on the hotel staff, nor am I a paying customer. My late father ran this hotel once, and when he sold it, I was given this corner to live in. It was part of the arrangement. I've been here most of my life, and believe me, there are stories to tell. Perhaps I should write a book too!'

But Mr Puri wasn't impressed. As far as he was concerned, there was only one author in the world worth reading, and that was Roshan Puri.

But he was right about the publisher. There was indeed one staying at the hotel: Cyrus Piranha, the genial, rotund owner of Chalta Hai Books.

Cyrus had made his fortune producing playing cards with erotic motifs and had got into trouble once or twice for flouting the obscenity laws. Now he was acquiring respectability by publishing 'literature'—mostly English translations of erotic Chinese, Japanese, Indian, Arabic and Madagascan classics. The fortune had doubled, and Cyrus usually took his holidays in Bermuda or Switzerland, where he had stashed away some of his wealth for a 'rainy day'. He was slumming in Mussoorie this time simply in order to please his wife who had once studied at Stockwood, one of the posh schools on the hillside.

Cyrus was not in the least interested in seeing an unpublished writer's first novel—he left such chores to his editors—but he was in a good mood, enjoying the climate and the company in the Royal's bar—so he smiled affably at the young man who thrust a manuscript into his lap and said, 'Here's your next bestseller, Mr Piranha. Read it while you are here—it will be an unforgettable experience!'

From then on, Cyrus's visit to Mussoorie became one long unforgettable experience.

Miss Ripley-Bean looked on with some amusement as the obsessed young writer went about stalking, and sometimes pouncing upon the unfortunate publisher.

Mr Piranha did, in fact, skim through the manuscript, but

the love scenes were obviously second-hand, lacking in masala, and he sent it across to Roshan Puri's room with a note saying, 'Not our kind of book. Why not try Champagne Press?'

Roshan had already tried Champagne Press, whose managing editor had recently been found strangled to death in one of those small guest houses that proliferate around Ansari Road, Daryaganj. In fact, Roshan had been rejected by almost every publisher in the capital. He had taken his revenge on quite a few of them; the publisher of Chalta Hai Books would not get off so easily!

A period of stalking ensued. Wherever Cyrus Piranha went, Roshan would follow, albeit at a discreet distance. Miss Ripley-Bean couldn't help noticing Roshan's agitation whenever he caught sight of the publisher ambling across the lawns and pathways surrounding the old hotel. The grounds were extensive and it could take about half an hour to circle the property on foot. She repeated to herself in an undertone:

Mary had a little lamb,
Its fleece as white as snow,
And everywhere that Mary went,
The lamb was sure to go.

'You are always quoting nursery rhymes,' observed Mr Lobo, joining Miss Ripley-Bean for a cup of tea.

'Great truths in nursery rhymes. They capture the spirit of the times.'

'Ancient times or modern times?'

'Both. Human beings haven't changed all that much. Greed and envy and love and hate continue to ride piggyback on our shoulders like the ghost in those tales of Vetaal.'

'And what happened to Mary's little lamb?'

'I'm not sure, probably turned into roast lamb with mint

sauce. Isn't that on the hotel's menu for today? A speciality of the Royal.'

Roshan Puri decided to make one final attempt at convincing Cyrus Piranha of the virtues and great potential of his book. Most writers see themselves as geniuses, even when others don't, and Roshan had greater conceit than most. And in his insane moments, had he not become a superhuman eliminating some unworthy members of the human race?

Cyrus Piranha went for a walk on that fateful day. Not too long a walk: around Camel's Back, past the cemetery and as far as Lover's Leap—a promontory on the edge of a cliff crowned by a hawa-ghar, an open pavilion where strollers could sit and gossip.

Hill station legend had it that a pair of young lovers, ostracized by society and driven from their homes, had committed suicide by leaping to their death from this particular spot. It was a long drop—about a hundred feet—to the rocks below. There was nothing by way of bushes or shrubbery to impede one's descent.

But that had been a long time ago, and in the recent past no one had made the leap.

It was a beautiful summer's day, and Miss Ripley-Bean had also gone for a walk, accompanied by Fluff. But they took the upper road, the path that went over the brow of the hill, past the old church and a disused tennis court. Resting there on a bench, she could see the road below and the pavilion at Lover's Leap.

There were no lovers in sight, just two men having a heated argument. Miss Ripley-Bean could make out Roshan Puri's high-pitched voice, raised in anger, but she could not make out what he was saying. The other man could be Cyrus Piranha, but Miss Ripley-Bean couldn't be sure because he stood in the shadows, his back to the pavilion wall. She could hear him laugh from time to time. Yes, it was Cyrus's boisterous laugh.

Suddenly, Roshan made a lunge at his tormentor, arms outstretched. The bigger man stepped back, raising his walking stick. He could not back away too much because the wall was behind him, but Roshan stood in the open, no wall or railing behind him. He was leaping about like a dervish, trying to get at Cyrus's throat. Cyrus kept him at bay with the walking stick. They moved back and forth, like a couple of sparring stag beetles. Then the walking stick shot out, catching Roshan in the midriff. He let out a howl, stepped back, slipped on a carpet of pine needles and went over the edge of the cliff.

A faint thud, and then silence. Two or three passers-by gathered at the spot, looked over the edge. Cyrus was busy explaining things. Down on the rocks a dead man lay, his vacant eyes staring up at the noonday sun. Did he fall or was he pushed? No one could be certain. Even Miss Ripley-Bean wasn't certain, but she hurried back to the hotel, Fluff at her heels, to inform Mr Lobo and others of the tragedy.

So it was all an accident, it appeared. And Roshan Puri had no family or close relatives to come poking around and making a fuss. There was a post-mortem of course, which listed the poor fellow's injuries, and as it was midsummer, the body was cremated without delay.

'Do you think he was the strangler?' Mr Lobo wondered. 'He seemed harmless enough.'

'Except for those large hands,' said Miss Ripley-Bean. 'And we shall know in time, depending on whether or not the population of Delhi publishers continues to decline...'

But Cyrus Piranha was still his jovial self. He had of course seen Miss Ripley-Bean on the hilltop that fatal day, but he wasn't sure just how much she had seen. Nor had she given him any indication of her thoughts or suspicions.

The day before he was due to leave, he presented her with a bottle of wine and asked her if there was anything he could do for her. It appeared that he had taken a liking to the old lady during his brief but eventful holiday.

'Well, there is something you *can* do for me,' said Miss Ripley-Bean after a moment's thought. 'You see, I'm writing this history of the hill station—the Queen of the Hills is over a hundred—and it's full of interesting people and things that have happened over the years. Famous visitors, memorable events, lovers' leaps, and even the odd murder... Well, it's time I started looking for a publisher.'

'Say no more, my good lady!' interrupted Cyrus. 'Consider me your publisher. My office will send you a contract, and before I go I will leave a small cheque with you by way of an advance.'

And true to his word, Cyrus presented Miss Ripley-Bean with a cheque for five thousand rupees, which at the time happened to be the highest advance ever received by a first-time author from a publisher in India.

And what happened to Roshan Puri's masterpiece? The forgotten manuscript lay in that unlucky, unoccupied room for several weeks, until one day the room-boy came across it, took it home, gave it to his friend who worked in the tea shop down the road, who gave it to the owner of the shop, who got his daughter to fashion paper bags out of those hundreds of foolscap pages, and then used the paper bags for selling peanuts and channa to his customers.

This, of course, was in the days before plastic bags came into use. And before frustrated geniuses could publish their masterpieces online!

THE LATE NIGHT SHOW

According to the crime novels I used to read, there there are four principal reasons for committing murder:

1. Money
2. Property
3. Revenge
4. Insanity, temporary or otherwise

In that order of priority.

But according to the crime movies I used to see, the priorities were a little different:

1. Passion (hate/jealousy)
2. Insanity (serial killing)
3. Money (bank hold-ups)
4. Espionage

Having grown up on crime fiction (both in literature and on film) I think my assessments are not far off the mark. When I put it to my friend Inspector Keemat Lal a few years ago, he said 50 per cent of murders were the result of greed—for money, property or another person's possessions. He was right, of course, but something as mundane as that doesn't make for great films or novels.

♦

In the year I finished school, I was still staying with my mother in the old Green's Hotel in Dehradun. Just across the road was the Odeon, a small cinema showing English and American films. Every winter, during the school holidays, I had been a regular picture-goer. Now that I had finished school, I was still a patron of the cinema, but preferred going to the night shows, from nine thirty to twelve. At night, the hall was usually half-empty, and the usher-cum-ticket-collector, who had become a friend of mine, would let me in without a ticket—provided I occupied one of the cheaper seats. As pocket money was in short supply (my mother's salary was both poor and irregular), I readily accepted my friend's assistance. In this way I saw almost every Hollywood or British film made around that period.

Just as much of my reading was centred around Agatha Christie, Ellery Queen and Edgar Wallace, so did my taste in films veer towards the slick thrillers in which stars such as James Cagney, Humphrey Bogart and Edward G. Robinson portrayed various colourful characters from the underworld. Back then, I remember how strange it felt watching these actors transition from their roles as gangsters or outlaws to portraying detective heroes (as Bogart did in *The Maltese Falcon*) or even appearing in musicals (like Cagney in *Yankee Doodle Dandy*).

If today I have an almost encyclopaedic knowledge of films made in the 1940s and 1950s, it is due largely to my usher friend who allowed me into the Odeon night after night, putting his job at some risk in doing so. I reciprocated by bringing him the occasional bottle of beer from the Green's bar. The barman, too, was a friend of mine.

There were other regulars who came to the night shows—salesmen, shopkeepers, waiters, those who did not get much time off during the day. And some old characters too—like the retired postmaster who never missed a film but always fell asleep after a couple of reels and whose snoring drowned out the sound from the projection room; or the hunchback who always sat in the front row because he couldn't see anything from the back; or the man who drank endless cups of tea throughout the show. Mostly menfolk. Women seldom came to the night show, unless escorted by husbands or family.

One regular always intrigued me. He was a man in his thirties who sat through the show without ever removing his hat. Presumably he was bald and felt the cold draught that ran through the hall whenever one of the doors were opened. In January the hall could be cold. He wore an overcoat too, which also served as a receptacle for packets of channa, which he munched assiduously during the film. Those were the days before fast foods of various descriptions took over. You had a choice between peanuts and channa. And apart from tea, there was a crimson-coloured cold drink called Vimto, which had a raspberry flavour. The gentleman with the hat always drank Vimto.

There was no social intercourse during the film. Either you saw the picture or you left the hall. The hatted gentleman almost always took the same seat, not far from one of the exit doors. Occasionally he would have a companion, but not for long. Mr Hat watched the film in its entirety, but the companions came and went. Sometimes he would offer them something from the folds of his overcoat. They would pocket the offering and leave after a few minutes.

One night there was a little more activity than usual in the row where Mr Hat was sitting. He came with a companion, who left after a few minutes. A little later he was joined by another person. I did not pay much attention to them and was engrossed in *The Third Man*, Anton Karas's haunting zither music building up to the chase in the sewers of Vienna, with

Joseph Cotten hunting down his black-marketeer friend Orson Welles. Cotten, not Welles, was my favourite actor.

The activity around Mr Hat was something of a distraction, and one or two in the hall shouted to them to shut up or go home. One of his companions, a tall individual, got up suddenly and walked towards the exit. He passed in front of me. And when he pushed open the door, the light from the foyer fell on his face and I caught a glimpse of narrow eyes, a large hooked nose, and a jutting chin. Then the door closed and I was back in the world of post-war Vienna. Ten minutes later the film was over and the lights came on. We began moving slowly out of the theatre—reluctantly, as it was freezing outside.

Mr Hat hadn't moved. He was hunched forward, his hat tilted over his head. I thought he'd fallen asleep. Curious as ever, I took a few steps down the central aisle and looked down at him. At first I thought he'd spilled a bottle of Vimto over his unbuttoned coat and shirt front. Then I realized that it was blood, not Vimto, that had gushed out of his torn and still bleeding throat. I cried out, and my usher friend came running. Then the manager. Then the tea-stall owner. Then those who were still in the hall.

'His throat's been cut,' said someone. 'He's dead or dying'

And by the time a policeman and a doctor arrived, Mr Hat's life-blood had seeped away.

◆

It was two or three weeks before I visited the Odeon again, and then too only for a matinée.

'No more night shows,' said my mother. 'You must be in the hotel by nine, and preferably in your bed.'

'But it had nothing to do with me,' I protested. 'He was just another film-goer.'

'No ordinary film-goer gets stabbed to death in the middle of a picture. Wasn't someone with him?'

'Sometimes. I didn't really notice.'

But I had noticed the tall, hawk-nosed man who had left before the show ended. I would recognize him again. But I did not tell my mother this.

With nothing much to do late in the evening I began hanging around the Green's Hotel bar, where the bartender, Melaram, often chatted to me if he wasn't too busy. I sat by myself in a corner of the large, dimly lit room, watching the customers and sipping a shandy. I would have preferred a beer, but my mother had given Melaram instructions to serve me with nothing stronger than shandy.

'A pity you can't go to the Odeon any more,' he said sympathetically. 'Not at night, anyway. Why don't you go to the afternoon shows?'

'The free pass was only for the night shows,' I told him. 'The hall is practically empty at night.'

'Not surprising, with people getting murdered in their seats.'

'It only happened once.'

'True... So how would you like to see a Hindi movie? You can come with me. We'll go to the Filmistan. Your mother won't mind.'

So Melaram took me to see an extravaganza called *Ali Baba aur Chalees Chor*, which was the sort of film Melaram enjoyed. All I remember is that it had a nifty little heroine called Shakeela, who was easy on the eye.

The following week we saw another film, and this time we were accompanied by my friend Sitaram, one of the room boys. We sat in the cheaper seats and clapped with the tonga-wallas and labourers whenever the dashing hero (Dilip Kumar) rescued the coy heroine (Nalini Jaywant) from the menacing villain (Pran, as usual).

As we left the cinema and were about to cross the road, I thought I saw the man who had passed me in the Odeon the night Mr Hat had been killed. He looked at me, hesitated for a moment, and then passed on. Had he recognized me?

'Someone you know?' asked Melaram at my side.

'That fellow who just passed,' I said. 'I think he was with the man who got killed that night.'

'Well, better keep quiet about it,' said Melaram. 'I think he's from one of the drug gangs. If you see him again, don't let him think you recognize him.'

♦

To my suprise, the next time I saw him was in the Green's bar. He strode in as though looking for someone, then shrugged, sat down on a bar stool and ordered a beer. I was in my dark corner and probably he would not have noticed me just then, had I not got up and left the room by the service door. I felt his eyes on me. I thought it best not to hang around, so went to my room (my mother had allowed me to use one of the smaller hotel rooms), locked the door, switched on the bed-light, and immersed myself in *Wuthering Heights*.

It was the right sort of book for such a night. Outside, a storm had broken, thunder rolled across the heavens, and the rain came rattling down on the corrugated tin roof. I read for an hour or two, then looked at my watch—given to me recently for having passed out of school. It was only eleven o'clock. I switched off the light and tried to sleep. Presently the thunder grew more distant, the rain lessened. A breeze sprang up, and a bunch of bougainvillea kept tapping against the window panes.

And then someone was tapping on my door.

A light tap to begin with, and then louder, more insistent.

'Who's there?' I called, but no one answered.

Had it been the night-watchman, or Sitaram at a loose end, they would have said something. Perhaps Sitaram up to tricks?

'Go to bed,' I called out. 'I'm sleepy.'

No answer. But after a little while, more knocking. Then silence. Then footsteps receding.

I switched on my bedside radio and lay awake, listening to popular songs that held no special meaning for me. But at least the radio was company. Finally I fell asleep, the music still playing.

It must have been towards dawn that I woke again. The radio was still on, but the station had gone off the air and there was a lot of static coming over the airwaves. I switched it off.

That tapping again. But now it came from the window, not the door.

I got up on my knees and drew aside the window curtain. There was a face pressed against the glass. An outside light fell upon it and made it look more hideous than it really was. The slit eyes, hooked nose and wide sensual mouth seemed more sinister than ever. Boris Karloff as Frankenstein couldn't have been more frightening.

The apparition smiled at me, and I let the curtain fall.

And then I did a foolish thing. I leapt out of bed, opened my door, and ran barefoot down the corridor, calling for Sitaram, Melaram, the chowkidar, anyone!

But no one came. It was the hour before dawn, and no one stirred.

I ran out on to the back verandah, and he was waiting there—Hook Nose was waiting. In his right hand he held a *kukri*, its blade shining in the lamplight.

I turned and ran into the wilderness behind the hotel. A path ran down the slope and into a tangle of jungle. I knew it well.

He was running after me, crashing clumsily through the

lantana, but I was faster than him, and I kept running until I came to an abandoned cowshed that stood at the edge of the jungle.

I did not enter it. He would have caught me there. Instead I crouched behind some bushes—and waited.

He was not long in coming. He stopped in front of the open door—the shed's only door—then stepped inside. I could hear him stumbling around in the dark.

I crept up to the door, pulled it shut, and slid the bolt in. It was an old door, but strong, made of deodar wood. There were no windows in the shed, just a small slit high up on the wall. Mr Hook Nose would have to break the door down in order to get out. He'd need an axe to do that. Already he was hammering away with his fists and cursing.

I left him to it, and returned to the hotel.

Dawn was breaking. A cock crowed near the kitchen outhouse, while an early riser emerged from his room, yelling for his morning tea.

♦

I went to Bareilly to spend a month with one of my aunts. There were no bookshops in Bareilly, and no English cinema, and I was soon restless and eager to return to Dehradun.

When I got down at the station, Sitaram was there to meet me.

He told me that Melaram had gone to a new and bigger hotel, and that Green's had a new but inexperienced bartender. He also brought me up to date on all the films that were running in town.

Was it fear, curiosity, a morbid fascination that took me down to the old cowshed that very afternoon? Somehow I had to know if Hook Nose had escaped, or if he was still there, now a bag of bones!

I had lunch with my mother, then said I was going for a walk—it was a bracing February afternoon in the Doon—and took the jungle path down to the shed.

It was still locked. Dared I open that door? Would the revenant of Hook Nose come rushing out at me? Worse still, would I find his remains putrefying in the dust?

Well, I had to find out.

I opened the door and stepped inside.

It was so dark I could hardly see anything. In the stale air there was the smell of muskrats and rotting vegetation. But nothing that I would describe as a human smell.

I looked around. Toadstools grew on the floor. There was a pile of wood in one corner. A large grey rat ran out from under the woodpile and out through the open door. No sign of Hook Nose anywhere. Either he'd escaped on his own or someone had set him free. I felt relieved, but also apprehensive. What if he came looking for me again?

That evening, as I emerged from my room, Sitaram took me by the hand and said, 'Come on, the bar's open. I'll get you a beer. No customers as yet.'

I was still a year under the legal limit for drinking in a bar, but that didn't stop me from perching on a bar stool while Sitaram went in search of something for me to eat.

The bartender had his back to me. When he turned, a bottle of Golden Eagle in his hands, received the shock of my life. It was Hook Nose!

I almost fell off my stool. My first impulse was to get up and run. But his face was expressionless. All he did was open the bottle and top up a glass with beer, and place it before me. Was it possible that he did not recognize me?

Sitaram was beckoning me to a table in a dark alcove.

I hurried towards him.

'Who's the new bartender?' I asked urgently.

'Don't know his name,' said Sitaram, speaking rapidly in Hindustani. 'I don't think he knows it himself. Your mother felt sorry for him and gave him the job. Somehow he'd got locked into that old shed behind the hotel. Must have been there for several days before he was found, just by chance, when we went there for some firewood—he'd had nothing to eat and drink, and he'd hurt his head trying to get out. Lost his memory. Couldn't remember a thing. Had nowhere to go. So your mother gave him a job. He goes about in a bit of a daze, but he's all right for serving drinks. Perhaps he'll start remembering things one of these days... Why are you looking worried? It's no concern of yours. Come on, finish your beer and we'll go to the pictures. I've got the night off. There's a new film with Nimmi in it. You like her, don't you?'

DEATH OF A FAMILIAR

When I learnt from a mutual acquaintance that my friend Sunil had been killed, I could not help feeling a little surprised, even shocked. Had Sunil killed somebody, it would not have surprised me in the least; he did not greatly value the lives of others. But for him to have been the victim was a sad reflection of his rapid decline.

He was twenty-one at the time of his death. Two friends of his had killed him, stabbing him several times with their knives. Their motive was said to have been revenge. Apparently he had seduced their wives. They had invited him to a bar in Meerut, had plied him with country liquor, and had then accompanied him out into the cold air of a December night. It was drizzling a little. Near the bridge over the canal, one of his companions seized him from behind, while the other plunged a knife first into his stomach and then into his chest. When Sunil slumped forward, the other friend stabbed him in the back. A passing cyclist saw the little group, heard a cry and a groan, saw a blade flash in the light from his lamp. He pedalled furiously into town, burst into the kotwali and roused the sergeant on duty. Accompanied by two constables, they ran to the bridge but found the area deserted. It was only as the rising sun drew an open wound across the sky that they found Sunil's body on the canal bank, his head and shoulders on the sand, his legs in running water.

The bar keeper was able to describe Sunil's companions, and they were arrested that same morning in their homes. They had not found time to get rid of their blood-soaked clothes. As they were not known to me, I took very little interest in the proceedings against them; but I understand that they have appealed against their sentences of life imprisonment.

I was in Delhi at the time of the murder, and it was almost a year since I had last seen Sunil. We had both lived in Shahganj and had left the place for jobs; I to work in a newspaper office, he in a paper factory owned by an uncle. It had been hoped that he would in time acquire a sense of responsibility and some stability of character. But I had known Sunil for over two years, and in that time it had been made abundantly clear that he had not been born to fit in with the conventions. And as for character, his had the stability of a grasshopper. He was forever in search of new adventures and sensations, and this appetite of his for every novelty led him into some awkward situations.

He was a product of Partition, of the frontier provinces, of Anglo-Indian public schools, of films Indian and American, of medieval India, knights in armour, hippies, drugs, sex magazines and the subtropical Terai. Had he lived in the time of the Moguls, he might have governed a province with saturnine and spectacular success. Being born into the twentieth century, he was but a juvenile delinquent.

It must be said to his credit that he was a delinquent of charm and originality. I realized this when I first saw him, sitting on the wall of the football stadium, his long legs—looking even longer and thinner because of the tight trousers he wore—dangling over the wall, his chappals trailing in the dust of the road, while his white bush-shirt lay open, unbuttoned, showing his smooth brown chest. He had a smile on his long face, which, with its high cheekbones, gave his cheeks a cavernous look, an impression of unrequited hunger.

We were both watching the wrestling. Two practice bouts were in progress—one between two thin, undernourished boys, and the other between the master of the *akhara* and a bearded Sikh who drove trucks for a living. They struggled in the soft mud of the wrestling pit, their well-oiled bodies glistening in the sunlight that filtered through a massive banyan tree. I had been standing near the akhara for a few minutes when I became conscious of the young man's gaze. When I turned round to look at him, he smiled satanically.

'Are you a wrestler, too?' he asked.

'Do I look like one?' I countered.

'No, you look more like an athlete,' he said. 'I mean a long-distance runner. Very thin.'

'I'm a writer. Like long-distance runners, most writers are very thin.'

'You're an Anglo-Indian, aren't you?'

'My family history is very complicated, otherwise I'd be delighted to give you all the details.'

'You could pass for a European, you know. You're quite fair. But you have an Indian accent.'

'An Indian accent is very similar to a Welsh accent,' I observed. 'I might pass for Welsh, but not many people in India have met Welshmen!'

He chuckled at my answer, then stared at me speculatively. 'I say,' he said at length, as though an idea of great weight and importance had occurred to him. 'Do you have any magazines with pictures of dames?'

'Well, I may have some old *Playboy*s. You can have them if you like.'

'Thanks,' he said, getting down from the wall. 'I'll come and fetch them. This wresting is boring, anyway.'

He slipped his hand into mine (a custom of no special significance), and began whistling snatches of Hindi film tunes and the latest American hits.

I was living at the time in a small flat above the town's main shopping centre. Below me there were shops, restaurants and a cinema. Behind the building lay a junkyard littered with the framework of vintage cars and broken-down tongas. I was paying thirty rupees a month for my two rooms, and sixty to the Punjabi restaurant where I took my meals. My earnings as a freelance writer were something like a hundred and fifty rupees a month, sufficient to enable me to make both ends meet, provided I remained in the backwater that was Shahganj.

Sunil (I had learnt his name during our walk from the stadium) made himself at home in my flat as soon as he entered it. He went through all my magazines, books and photographs with the thoroughness of an executor of a will. In India, it is customary for people to try and find out all there is to know about you, and Sunil went through the formalities with considerable thoroughness. While he spoke, his roving eyes made a mental inventory of all my belongings. These were few—a typewriter, a small radio and a cupboard full of books and clothes, besides the furniture that went with the flat. I had no valuables. Was he disappointed? I could not be sure. He wore good clothes and spoke fluent English, but good clothes and good English are no criteria for honesty. He was a little too glib to inspire confidence. Apparently, he was still at college. His father owned a cloth shop—a strict man who did not give his son much spending money.

But Sunil was not seriously interested in money, as I was shortly to discover. He was interested in experience, and searched for it in various directions.

'You have a nice view,' he said, leaning over my balcony and looking up and down the street. 'You can see everyone on parade. Girls! They're becoming quite modern now. Short hair and small blouses. Tight salwars. Maxis, minis. Falsies. Do you like girls?'

'Well...' I began, but he did not really expect an answer to his question.

'What are little girls made of? That's an English poem, isn't it? "Sugar and spice and everything nice..." And I don't remember the rest.' He lowered his voice to a confidential undertone. 'Have you had any girls?'

'Well...'

'I had fun with a girl, you know, my cousin. She came to stay with us last summer. Then there's a girl in college who's stuck on me. But this is such a backward country. We can't be seen together in public and I can't invite her to my house. Can I bring her here some day?'

'Well, I don't know...' I hadn't lived in a small town like Shahganj for some time, and wasn't sure if morals had changed along with the fashions.

'Oh, not now,' he said. 'There's no hurry. I'll give you plenty of warning, don't worry.' He put an arm around my shoulders and looked at me with undisguised affection. 'We are going to be great friends, you and I.'

After that I began to receive almost daily visits from Sunil. His college classes got over at three in the afternoon, and though it was seldom that he attended them, he would stop at my place after putting in a brief appearance at the study hall. I could hardly blame him for neglecting his books: Shakespeare and Chaucer were prescribed for students who had but a rudimentary knowledge of modern English usage. Vast numbers of graduates were produced every year, and most of them became clerks or bus conductors or, perhaps, schoolteachers. But Sunil's father wanted the best for his son. And in Shahganj that meant as many degrees as possible.

Sunil would come stamping into my rooms, waking me from the siesta that had become a habit during summer afternoons. When he found that I did not relish being woken up, he would leave me to sleep while he took a bath under the tap. After making liberal use of my hair cream and aftershave lotion (he had just begun shaving, but used the lotion on his body), he would want to go to a picture or restaurant, and would sprinkle me with cold water so that I leapt off the bed.

One afternoon he felt more than usually ebullient, and poured a whole bucket of water over me, soaking the sheets and mattress. I retaliated by flinging the water jug at his head. It missed him and shattered itself against the wall. Sunil then went berserk and started splashing water all over the room, while I threatened and shouted. When I tried restraining him by force, we rolled over on the ground, and I banged my head against the bedstead and almost lost consciousness. He was then full of contrition and massaged the lump on my head with hair cream and refused to borrow any money from me that day.

Sunil's 'borrowing' consisted of extracting a few rupees from my wallet, saying he needed the money for books or a tailor's bill or a shopkeeper who was threatening him with violence, and then spending it on something quite different. Before long I gave up asking him to return anything, just as I had given up asking him to stop seeing me.

Sunil was one of those people best loved from a distance. He was born with a special talent for trouble. I think it pleased his vanity when he was pursued by irate creditors, shopkeepers, brothers whose sisters he had insulted and husbands whose wives he had molested. My association with him did nothing to improve my own reputation in Shahganj.

My landlady, a protective, motherly Punjabi widow said:

'Son, you are in bad company. Do you know that Sunil has already been expelled from one school for stealing, and from another for sexual offences?'

'He's only a boy,' I said. 'And he's taking longer than most boys to grow up. He doesn't realize the seriousness of what he does. He will learn as he grows older.'

'If he grows older,' said my landlady darkly. 'Do you know that he nearly killed a man last year? When a fruit seller who had been cheated threatened to report Sunil to the police, he threw a brick at the man's head. The poor man was in hospital for three weeks. If Sunil's father did not have political influence, the boy would be in jail now, instead of climbing your stairs every afternoon.'

Once again I suggested to Sunil that he come to see me less often.

He looked hurt and offended. 'Don't you like me any more?'

'I like you immensely. But I have work to do...'

'I know. You think I am a crook. Well, I am a crook.' He spoke with all the confidence of a young man who has never been hurt or disillusioned; he had romantic notions about swindlers and gangsters. 'I'll be a big crook one day, and people will be scared of me. But don't worry, old boy, you're my friend. I wouldn't harm you in any way. In fact, I'll protect you.'

'Thank you, but I don't require protection, I want to be left alone. I have work, and you are a worry and a distraction.'

'Well, I'm not going to leave you alone,' he said, assuming the posture of a spoilt child. 'Why should you be left alone? Who do you think you are? If we're friends now, it's your fault. I'm not going to buzz off just to suit your convenience.'

'Come less often, that's all.'

'I'll come more often, you old snob! I know, you're thinking of your reputation—as if you had any. Well, you don't have to worry, *mon ami*—as they say in Hollywood. I'll be very discreet, Daddy-ji!'

Whenever I complained or became querulous, Sunil would call me daddy or uncle or sometimes mum, and make me feel more ridiculous. If he was in a good mood, he would use the Hindi word chacha (uncle). All it did was to make me feel much older than my twenty-five years.

Sunil turned up one afternoon with blood streaming from his nose and from a gash across his forehead. He sat down at the foot of the bed and began dabbing his face with the bedsheet.

'What have you done to yourself?' I asked in some alarm.

'Some fellows beat me up. There were three of them. They followed me on their cycles.'

'Who were they?' I asked, looking for iodine on the dressing table.

'Just some fellows...'

'They must have had a reason.'

'Well, a sister of one of them had been talking to me.'

'Well, that isn't a reason, even in Shahganj. You must have said or done something to offend her.'

'No, she likes me,' he said, wincing as I dabbed iodine on his forehead. 'We went to the guava orchard near my uncle's farm.'

'She went out there alone with you?'

'Sure. I took her on my bike. They must have followed us. Anyway, we weren't doing much except kissing and fooling around. But some people seem to think that's worse than...'

Both he and the other boys of Shahganj had grown up to look upon girls as strange, exotic animals, who must be seized at the first opportunity. Experimenting in sex was like playing a surreptitious game of marbles.

Sunil produced a clasp knife from his pocket, opened it and held the blade against the flat of his hand.

'Don't worry, Uncle, I can look after myself. The next fellow who tries to interfere with me will get this in his guts.'

'Don't be silly,' I said. 'You will go to prison for ten years. Listen, I'm going up to Shimla for a couple of weeks, just for a change. Why don't you come with me? It will be a pleasant change from Shahganj, and in the meantime all this fuss will die down.'

It was one of those invitations that I make so readily and instantly regret. As soon as I had made the suggestion, I realized that Sunil in Shimla might be even more of a problem than Sunil in Shahganj. But it was too late for me to back out.

'Shimla! Why not? The college is closing for the summer holidays, and my father won't mind my going with you. He believes you're the only respectable friend I've got. Boy! We'll have a good time in Shimla.'

'You'll have to behave yourself there, if you want to come with me. No girls, Sunil.'

'No girls, Sir. I'll be very good, Chacha-ji. Please take me to Shimla.'

'I think two hundred rupees should be enough for a fortnight for both of us,' I said.

'Oh, too much,' said Sunil modestly.

And a week later we were actually in Shimla, putting up at a moderately priced, middle-class hotel.

Our first few days in the hill station were pleasant enough. We went for long walks, tired ourselves out and acquired enormous appetites. Sunil, in the hills for the first time in his life, declared that they were wonderful, and thanked me a score of times for bringing him along. He took a genuine interest in exploring remote valleys, forests and waterfalls, and seemed to be losing some of his self-centredness. I believe that mountains do affect one's personality, if one can remain among them long enough; and if Sunil had grown up in the hills instead of in a refugee township, I have no doubt he would have been a completely different person.

There was one small waterfall I rather liked. It was down a ravine, in a rather inaccessible spot, where very few people ever went. The water fell about thirty feet into a small pool. We bathed here on two occasions, and Sunil quite forgot the attractions of the town. And we would have visited the spot again had I not slipped and sprained my ankle. This accident confined me to the hotel balcony for several days, and I was afraid that Sunil, for want of companionship, would go in search of more mundane distractions. But though he went out often enough, he came back dusty and sunburnt; and the fact that he asked me for very little money was evidence enough of his fondness for the outdoors. Striding through forests of oak and pine, with all the world stretched out far below, was no doubt a new and exhilarating experience for him. But how long would it be before the spell was broken?

'Don't you need any money?' I asked him uneasily, on the third day of his Thoreau-like activities.

'What for, Uncle? Fresh air costs nothing. And besides, I don't owe money to anyone in Shimla. We haven't been here long enough.'

'Then perhaps we should be going,' I said.

'Shahganj is a miserable little dump.'

'I know, but it's your home. And for the time being, it's mine.'

'Listen, Uncle,' he said, after a moment of reflection, 'yesterday, on one of my walks, I met a schoolteacher. She's over thirty, so don't get nervous. She doesn't have any brothers or relatives who will come chasing after me. And she's much fairer than you, Uncle. Is it all right if I'm friendly with her?'

'I suppose so,' I said uncertainly. Schoolteachers can usually take care of themselves (if they want to), and, besides, an older woman might have a sobering influence on Sunil.

He brought her over to see me that same evening, and seemed quite proud of his new acquisition. She was indeed fair, perhaps insipidly so, with blonde hair and light blue eyes. She had a young face and a healthy body, but her voice was peculiarly toneless and flat, giving an impression of boredom, of lassitude. I wondered what she found attractive in Sunil apart from his obvious animal charm. They had hardly anything in common, but perhaps the absence of similar interests was an attraction in itself. In six or seven years of teaching, Maureen must have been tired of the usual scholastic types. Sunil was refreshingly free from all classroom associations.

Maureen let her hair down at the first opportunity. She switched on the bedroom radio and found Ceylon. Soon she was teaching Sunil to dance. This was amusing, because Sunil, with his long legs, had great difficulty in taking small steps; nor could Maureen cope with his great strides. But he was very earnest about it all, and inserting an unlighted cigarette between his lips, did his best to move rhythmically around the bedroom. I think he was convinced that by learning to dance he would reach the high watermark of Western culture. Maureen stood for all that was remote and romantic, and for all the films that he had seen; to conquer her would, for Sunil, be a voyage of discovery, not a mere gratification of his senses. And for Maureen, this new unconventional friendship must have been a refreshing diversion from the dreariness of her school routine. She was old enough to realize that it was only a diversion. The intensity of emotional attachments had faded with her early youth and love could wound her heart no more. But for Sunil, it was only the beginning of something that stirred him deeply, moved him inexorably towards manhood.

It was unfortunate that I did not then notice this subtle change in my friend. I had known him only as a shallow creature, and was certain that this new infatuation would disappear as soon as the novelty of it wore off. As Maureen had no encumbrances, no relations that she would speak of, I saw no harm in encouraging the friendship and seeing how it would develop.

'I think we'd better have something to drink,' I said, and ringing the bell for the room bearer, ordered several bottles of beer.

Sunil gave me an odd, whimsical look. I had never before encouraged him to drink. But he did not hesitate to open the bottles, and, before long, Maureen and he were drinking from the same glass.

'Let's make love,' said Sunil, putting his arm around-Maureen's shoulders and gazing adoringly into her dreamy blue eyes.

They seemed unconcerned by my presence; but I was embarrassed, and, getting up, said I would be going for a walk.

'Enjoy yourself,' said Sunil, winking at me over Maureen's shoulder.

'You ought to get yourself a girlfriend,' said the young woman in a conciliatory tone.

'True,' I said, and moved guiltily out of the room I was paying for.

Our stay in Shimla lasted several days longer than we had planned. I saw little of Sunil and Maureen during this time. As Sunil had no desire to return to Shahganj any earlier than was absolutely necessary, he avoided me during the day but I managed to stay awake late enough one night to confront him when he crept quietly into the room.

'Dear friend and familiar,' I said. 'I hate to spoil your beautiful romance, but I have absolutely no money left, and unless you have resources of your own—or if Maureen can support you—I suggest that you accompany me back to Shahganj the day after tomorrow.'

'How mean you are, Chacha-ji. This is something serious. I mean Maureen and me. Do you think we should get married?'

'No.'

'But why not?'

'Because she cannot support you on a teacher's salary. And she probably isn't interested in a permanent relationship—like ours.'

'Very funny. And you think I'd let my wife slave for me?'

'I do. And besides…'

'And besides,' he interrupted, grinning, 'she's old enough to be my mother.'

'Are you really in love with her?' I asked him. 'I've never known you to be serious about anything.'

'Honestly, Uncle.'

'And what about her?'

'Oh, she loves me terribly, really she does. She's ready to come down with us if it's possible. Only I've told her that I'll first have to break the news to my father, otherwise he might kick me out of the house.'

'Well, then,' I said shrewdly, 'the sooner we return to Shahganj and get your father's blessings, the sooner you and Maureen can get married, if that's what both of you really want.'

Early next morning Sunil disappeared, and I knew he would be gone all day. My foot was better, and I decided to take a walk on my own to the waterfall I had liked so much. It was almost noon when I reached the spot and began descending the steep path to the ravine. The stream was hidden by dense foliage, giant ferns and dahlias, but the water made a tremendous noise as it tumbled over the rocks. When I reached a sharp promontory, I was able to look down on the pool. Two people were lying on the grass.

I did not recognize them at first. They looked very beautiful together, and I had not expected Sunil and Maureen to look so beautiful. Sunil, on whom no surplus flesh had as yet gathered, possessed all the sinuous grace and power of a young god; and the woman, her white flesh pressed against young grass, reminded me of a painting by Titian that I had seen in a gallery in Florence. Her full, mature body was touched with a tranquil intoxication, her breasts rose and fell slowly, and waves of muscle merged into the shadows of her broad thighs. It was as though I had stumbled into another age, and had found two lovers in a forest glade. Only a fool would have wished to disturb them. Sunil had for once in his life risen above mediocrity, and I hurried away before the magic was lost.

The human voice often shatters the beauty of the most tender passions; and when we left Shimla the next day, and Maureen and Sunil used all the stock cliches to express their love, I was a little disappointed. But the poetry of life was in their bodies, not in their tongues.

Back in Shahganj, Sunil actually plucked up the courage to speak to his father. This, to me, was a sign that he took the affair very seriously, for he seldom approached his father for anything. But all the sympathy that he received was a box on the ears. I received a curt note suggesting that I was having a corrupting influence on the boy and that I should stop seeing him. There was little I could do in the matter, because it had always been Sunil who had insisted on seeing me.

He continued to visit me, bring me Maureen's letters (strange, how lovers cannot bear that the world should not know their love), and his own to her, so that I could correct his English!

It was at about this time that Sunil began speaking to me about his uncle's paper factory and the possibility of working in it. Once he was getting a salary, he pointed out, Maureen would be able to leave her job and join him.

Unfortunately, Sunil's decision to join the paper factory took months to crystallize into a definite course of action, and in the meantime he was finding a panacea for lovesickness in rum and sometimes cheap country spirit. The money that he now borrowed was used not to pay his debts, or to incur new ones, but to drink himself silly. I regretted having been the first person to have offered him a drink. I should have known that Sunil was a person who could do nothing in moderation.

He pestered me less often now, but the purpose of his occasional visits became all too obvious. I was having a little success, and thoughtlessly gave Sunil the few rupees he usually demanded. At the same time I was beginning to find other friends, and I no longer found myself worrying about Sunil, as I had so often done in the past. Perhaps this was treachery on my part...

When finally I decided to leave Shahganj for Delhi, I went in search of Sunil to say goodbye. I found him in a small bar, alone at a table with a bottle of rum. Though barely twenty, he no longer looked a boy. He was a completely different person from the handsome, cocksure youth I had met at the wrestling pit a year previously. His cheeks were hollow and he had not shaved for days. I knew that when I first met him he had been without scruples, a shallow youth, the product of many circumstances. He was no longer so shallow and he had stumbled upon love, but his character was too weak to sustain the weight of disillusionment. Perhaps I should have left him severely alone from the beginning. Before me sat a ruin, and I had helped to undermine the foundations. None of us can really avoid seeing the outcome of our smallest actions...

'I'm off to Delhi, Sunil.'

He did not look up from the table.

'Have a good time,' he said.

'Have you heard from Maureen?' I asked, certain that he had not.

He nodded, but for once did not offer to show me the letter.

'What's wrong?' I asked.

'Oh, nothing,' he said, looking up and forcing a smile. 'These dames are all the same, Uncle. We shouldn't take them too seriously, you know.'

'Why, what has she done, got married to someone else?'

'Yes,' he said scornfully. 'To a bloody teacher.'

'Well, she wasn't young,' I said. 'She couldn't wait for you forever, I suppose.'

'She could if she had really loved me. But there's no such thing as love, is there, Uncle?'

I made no reply. Had he really broken his heart over a woman? Were there, within him, unsuspected depths of feeling and passion? You find love when you least expect to and lose it when you are sure that it is in your grasp.

'You're a lucky beggar,' he said. 'You're a philosopher. You find a reason for every stupid thing and so you are able to ignore all stupidity.'

I laughed. 'You're becoming a philosopher yourself. But don't think too hard, Sunil, you might find it painful.'

'Not I, Chacha-ji,' he said, emptying his glass. 'I'm not going to think. I'm going to work in a paper factory. I shall become respectable. What an adventure that will be!'

And that was the last time I saw Sunil.

He did not become respectable. He was still searching like a great discoverer for something new, someone different, when he met his pitiful end in the cold rain of a December night.

Though murder cases usually get reported in the papers, Sunil was a person of such little importance that his violent end was not considered newsworthy. It went unnoticed, and

Maureen could not have known about it. The case has already been forgotten, for in the great human mass that is India, hundreds of people disappear every day and are never heard of again. Sunil will be quickly forgotten by all except those to whom he owed money.

www.ingramcontent.com/pod-product-compliance
Lightning Source LLC
Chambersburg PA
CBHW031123020726
47495CB00007B/2325